Terry Richardson was born in the Somerset village of Baltonsborough in 1941; moving to London when a teenager in 1959. Retiring from the railway in 1999 after almost thirty years service, he and his wife moved back to Somerset. They now live in a village on the Somerset Levels about fifteen miles from his original home. When visiting family and friends who still live in the Baltonsborough area, they of course talked about the escapades and scrapes they had as kids. The result is this book which although primarily for children could also bring back memories for many people who were lucky enough to have a childhood in that era.

TWO T'S

Terry Richardson

Two T's

Vanguard Press

VANGUARD PAPERBACK

© Copyright 2005
Terry Richardson

A CIP catalogue record for this title is
available from the British Library
ISBN 1 84386 149 6

Illustrations By Stephen Honey

*Vanguard Press is an imprint of
Pegasus Elliot MacKenzie Publishers Ltd.*
www.pegasuspublishers.com

First Published in 2005

**Vanguard Press
Sheraton House Castle Park
Cambridge England**

Printed & Bound in Great Britain

Dedication

To my wife, Margaret for her total support over the many years it has taken me to write this book. When I thought I would never get it published her unstinting belief in the merits of this work kept me going.

Thank you Margaret

The troublesome twosome or Two T's as Tom and Timmy are often called, is the story of two boys growing up in a Somerset village

Exasperating to their parents, teachers and almost all adults they came into contact with, Tom and Timmy are the type of boys you might like to read about, but hope not to meet. These two friends with a sense of fun, imagination and a resourcefulness to match, could turn almost any situation into an adventure. The adventures, more often than not had disastrous consequences; but this did not seem to deter them as they blithely went from one little scrape to the next. The stories, set in the middle of the last century, are told by an old man to his grandchildren and are mostly humorous, sometimes even hilarious. They become more poignant though when Timmy is taken ill and is incarcerated in a sanatorium on the Mendip Hills. Oh, how he hated it. As he got better Timmy began to resent his internment and lost freedom. With his returning well-being and sense of fun, the rebellious escapades that followed are probably the most outrageous in this book.

Unashamedly a boy's book
Age 9-99

Contents

Friends for Life   15
Sneeze the Sailing Dog   20
Apples, Moles and Darn Cows   25
The Wrath of Mrs Vicar   36
Goats   49
The Ghosts of Orchard House   53
The Orangy Red Bike   63
The Shrinking Sledge   79
The Old Man of the Moors   96
Plums   109
The Marquee   118
Interned   123
Interned (Part 2)   139
Home   162

Friends for Life

"A penny for them Granddad," said Stuart as he and his brother climbed up the bank from the Mill Stream, where they had been poking about and throwing stones. "You haven't moved a muscle for ages."

"I was thinking of a drama that happened on the other side of this pool many years ago." came the reply. "Is this going to be one of your stories Granddad?" said Stuart

expectantly as he and James settled down on the grass just below him. "I don't think this little story has ever been told properly," said the grandfather. "It's about two little boys who at the time were probably younger than you are now." his voice trailing away, so that James and Stuart had to lean forward to catch his words.

"It was summer in the late forties or early fifties. They were two village urchins of nine or ten and had a freedom not many youngsters of today can enjoy. The two boys had known each other for as long as they could remember. Although there were other friends in the village; Tom and

Timmy seemed to do most things together. The morning had started bright and sunny; both had felt a sense of excitement as they made ready to go fishing. The excitement was not only because of the fishing trip, though fishing was one of their favourite pastimes, it was because today was the first day of the summer holidays. Six weeks was too long for Timmy to contemplate, the school holiday would last an eternity; stretching away in front of him was the whole of the summer in which he and Tom could do as they liked. Life could not be better.

Into their fishing bags, along with hooks, floats, bait and other fishing paraphernalia had gone bread, cheese, jam sandwiches and bottles of water; because this was to be an all day expedition. Tom was a sturdy lad with quite a fine fishing rod; Timmy on the other hand, was almost painfully thin and had a homemade rod of cane. Tom's father was a keen fisherman; hence the good rod. Timmy's dad, a proud little Cockney, had been a Sergeant PT Instructor before his demob from the army and his interest in country sports was almost zilch. With the advent of war, the family had been evacuated to the village from London, but could not return when it was all over, because the family home had been blitzed. Timmy, who had been born in the village, sometimes wore glasses, that is if they were not lost or broken, as was quite often the case.

His frustrated mother would cry. "Where are your glasses?" as he tramped in for his evening meal. This was probably the first time she had seen him for hours. "It's a good job that boy gets hungry," she had said several times to his sisters, "If not we probably wouldn't see him for days."

When accosted in this way Timmy would put his hands to his face and then on top of his head, because quite often his glasses were there, but obviously they were not because his mother would have seen them. Exasperatingly she would talk him through all the places he had been that day and where the spectacles might have been lost, or where he might have put them down. He quite often took them off and put them down for safe keeping and then forgot them. Sometimes they were lucky and he managed to retrieve them, but more often than not, the glasses were lost for good. Timmy had made his own fishing rod and was quite pleased with it, though he would of course, have liked a rod such as Tom's. With his father's tuition Tom was a better fisherman than Timmy, and even though he knew this, Timmy would not admit it to Tom or anyone else; anyway fishing was only one of their many pastimes or activities. They were fishing for whatever would take the bait and the bait was mostly worms dug from the garden, or bread made into dough or even a bit of cheese, if it was not eaten before it got on the hook. As for the fish, there were perch, bass, eels and some fine chub. On one memorable day Tom had caught a trout and eaten it for his tea. By about the middle of the day the early morning excitement had worn off. For all their skills and knowledge of this little river, today the fish would not bite. Timmy was down at the edge of the bank overlooking one of the many pools still trying to catch fish. Tom, having tired of trying to catch this unobliging prey, was sitting on the top of the bank and was now looking for other ways of amusing himself.

"I'm going to roll down on top of you." He said. "Well if you do, you'll fall in the river." replied Timmy. "If I go in so will you," And with that Tom rolled down. Though Timmy was thin, he was wiry and he hung on to the grass, and was not dislodged by Tom, who went over the top of him and landed with a splash in the river. Now, this might seem strange but neither of these country boys could swim. Over the years they would have had lots of opportunities to learn to swim, but somehow it had never happened. For a grown man that could not swim this pool would hold little danger, but, to a nine year old it might as well be twenty feet deep. Timmy shouted and screamed his friend's name and then screamed for help, for he knew how deep the water was that he had just been fishing in, but there was no help forthcoming. They had not seen another soul on either of the river banks and the nearest house was well out of shouting distance. As for Tom he was now near the middle of the pool and was trying to

climb onto the weed, which was in abundance in this little river, but of course it would not hold him up. Timmy used his homemade rod, and somehow, neither could remember how, Tom managed to get to the bank. But, their trouble was far from over. At some time in the past, there had been a bank slip and now the last five or six feet of the bank was almost vertical, with very little vegetation growing on it. With Timmy holding on to the grass and leaning over as far as he could and Tom stretching up as far as he could, they managed to hold hands. Now the struggle began, and what a struggle it was for these two small boys. They do not know how long they hung there, with Tom trying to get a hold on this now very wet and slippery riverbank, and Timmy doing all he could to pull him up. At last, Tom managed to get his free hand over the lip and held on to the grass, but by now they were both utterly exhausted. Their heads side by side but in opposite directions they just hung in this position, too tired to move and not enough strength to do any more. Tom seemed to be sliding back down the bank; he looked at his friend and actually said, "Goodbye." Can you believe a boy of nine or ten saying something like that? But it certainly did something to Timmy.

"NO! NO! NO!" He screamed. This frenzy seemed to give them a little extra strength and somehow or other Tom was over the lip and they were crawling to the top of the bank. When they had recovered, hardly a word was spoken, they were shaken and a little in awe of what had just taken place. They had been involved in scrapes in the past and would have many adventures in the future, but each was aware that they would remember this event for the rest of their lives. Although they told their parents and others, only they knew what they had really gone through. They remained friends for many years, but both moved from their native village. Tom went to live in New Zealand but, on a recent visit back to England, one of the first things he did was to make a pilgrimage to this little pool. Timmy has done the same several times, always on his own… Until now.

Sneeze the Sailing Dog

"Granddad, GRANDDAD, GRANDDAD!" Shouted Stuart.

The old man stirred, shaking his head with a slightly bemused look on his face.

"Sorry lads I was deep in thought."

"We know that Granddad." laughed James, "But while your mind is back on those two boys, maybe you can remember what other adventures they got up to? You did say they had lots of them."

"Well as a matter of fact I can," said the grandfather. "Before you so rudely broke into my reflections, I was thinking of another little scrape they got into on this same stream."

The Troublesome Twosome, or Two T's as Tom and Timmy were often called could now swim. After their recent escapade when Tom had almost drowned, they had been told they could not go near the river or on to the moors until they could swim. The boys had really put some effort into learning and with the help of Tom's elder cousin, were now quite proficient swimmers. On this early evening after school, and with a younger friend, they were wading in the water, down stream of the mill. The trio were catching eels, though not with a fishing rod. Their method of fishing was rather unorthodox, but was as simple as it was effective. In the summer, or a period of time when there was little rain, the hatches or sluice gates controlling the water to the mill would be closed. The bypass hatches would also be closed by the miller so that a head of water could be built up to drive the mill. This would sometimes take several hours and in the meantime the water in the stretch of the stream below the mill was then only a foot or so deep, though a few pools were quite a bit deeper. Armed with a table fork, the stones on the bottom were gently turned over by the fishermen and if this exposed an eel it was stabbed with the fork. A lot of people did not like doing this because the eel would then wrap itself around your wrist and arm. Timmy was a real expert at this. Although he now lived in one of the new council houses, he had been born only a few yards away in a big old thatched house, where the water of this stream actually brushed along one wall. He used to be able to fish out of the kitchen window.

Their friend John was almost inseparable with his delightfully scruffy little dog called Sneeze. Sneeze followed the fishermen along the bank, the water being too deep for him. All was well until they came to a field with cows in it. These beasts are very curious and they pestered the poor little dog. The boys chased them off now and again, but they kept coming back. It was then that they came across a tin bath hidden under a bush. The tin bath was kept by the stream for use in another type of eel fishing called Radballing. In other parts of the country it is probably called something else. The bath would have a piece of string attached and then floated on the water. A long pole with a piece of springy metal on the end, normally an old pail handle, would have a bunch of wool-strung worms attached. This was then plunged under the bank or in the mud. When the eels tried to take the worms, the fisherman would feel them tugging; the pole was then lifted out of the water and the eels shook off into the bath. It was Tom's idea to float the bath and put the dog in it, it wobbled about a bit so a few stones were added for ballast. Sneeze seemed to love it, having a good old bark at the cows now that they could not get at him. They had almost come to the end of this stretch of the stream when John noticed the water was rising. The boys scrambled out on to the bank because when the mill started or the bypass hatches were opened, the water below the mill rose several

feet within seconds. While sitting on the bank emptying the water out of their wellingtons, one of them realised the dog was still in the bath and the bath was now careering down the river at a great rate of knots, as they watched, it disappeared under the road bridge. They gave chase but it was a long time before they caught up with it and when they did there was not much to be done, except run along the bank and hope it would come to the side. Sneeze thought this was a new game and seemed to thoroughly enjoy it, barking all the time and jumping about so much he almost tipped the bath up. At last the Mill Stream met with the main river. At this junction where the two rivers met, was a tree with branches hanging low over the water and on these branches the bath stuck. It was well out of reach and the current was still quite fast. John tried climbing along the branch but it dipped into the water and almost turned the bath over.

"What we need," said Timmy, "is a long stick with some sort of hook on it so we can drag it to the bank." Although a thorough search of the area was made nothing came to hand that that could be utilised, so it was decided to look further afield. John stayed to keep the dog company, Timmy went down stream and Tom went back the way they had come. Timmy found a branch from a tree he thought would do but when he got back he found it was too short, so they sat down and waited for Tom. By now Sneeze was fed up with this game and was whimpering. Every so often he would give a really big howl.

"He is a stupid dog," said Timmy, "Why doesn't he just jump out and swim?" John thought the current was too strong. He was almost in tears, Sneeze was his best friend. At last Tom arrived with a very long pole and it was just the job. He was a bit evasive about where it had come from but the other two did not worry about that. It was even forked on the end so when it was put though the handle of the bath and turned, it did not slip out. In just a few minutes the bath and dog were rescued. The way Sneeze and John acted you would think they had been apart for months.

"What are you going to do with the pole?" said Timmy. "I don't know, throw it away I suppose." said Tom. "Well if you don't want it I'll have it," said Timmy. "There must be lots of uses for a pole like that, I'll take it home." "I would leave it here if I were you" replied Tom as he hid the bath under a bush for future use. "It won't be any good for anything." But Timmy wanted that pole and it was on his shoulder when they set off for home. Tom went on ahead and was soon out of sight of the other two.

"I wonder why he's in such a hurry?" said Timmy as they neared the first house of the village.

"You little wretch," said a voice from the other side of the stream. They turned to see a woman with a very red face shaking her fist. "You little wretch, give me back my clothes prop." Timmy knew where the pole had come from now, he also knew why Tom had gone on in front. The woman was seething as Timmy leaned over the stream to give her prop back. He thought if she falls in I can rescue her, then I'll be a hero. When she had hold of the end of the prop he was almost tempted to give it a tug. Thank goodness he didn't. He noticed with interest she had now gone from red to white with a quivering rage, almost as white as her sheets that were hanging on the droopy clothes line, except for the ends which were dangling in the mud. When he turned to leave John and Sneeze had gone, they had scarpered. As he climbed over the gate to get out onto the road she shouted.

"I'll be seeing your mother shortly." And she did, and he was grounded for a while.

"You wait till I see that Tom." muttered Timmy as he cleared up his bedroom, the first of many chores he had to do while he was grounded.

Apples, Moles and Darn Cows

"I quite liked that story, Granddad," said James, "I can imagine that dog careering down the river in an old bath. But were all their adventures on the river?"

"Oh no." replied the old man, "Although the river drew them like a magnet, their escapades ranged over the whole locality and later, when they obtained bicycles, nowhere in the county was safe from their exploits.

"So can you think of anything else they got up to then Granddad?" said Stuart; hoping the stories were not going to dry up.

"Of course I can; when I cast my mind back the stories seem almost limitless, because those boys were always up to something. I am now just remembering the episode of the moles."

"Moles Granddad? said James. "How can you have a story about moles? They're just tiny little insignificant furry things; you don't even see them, only the hills they make like the ones on mums lawn."

"Well, just you listen young man and you might learn something."

David was trying to sell Timmy his Mole Traps, but this was a waste of time because Timmy didn't have any money. His meagre pocket money was spent on the same day as he got it. At certain times of the year he could supplement his allowance by blackberry picking, hay making, apple picking, or even collecting mistletoe in December, but March was not a good month. This was the reason that Timmy was interested in the traps. He had been told there was good money to be made from mole trapping; whatever good money was, he didn't know. All he knew was, he didn't have any. Timmy had never seen mole traps before and did not even know how they worked. David, who lived with his family on a small farm about a mile outside the village, took Timmy down the end of the lane and into one of his father's fields. This field had a few mole hills and Timmy was given a demonstration and shown the finer arts of mole catching. This really wetted Timmy's appetite and he was determined to raise the money to buy those mole traps. With the demonstration over they walked back to the farm. The two were in a real heated discussion over prices and terms as they passed the first cottage, which lay a long way back from the road. David normally tried to keep well clear of this cottage, but his animated conversation and intense debate with Timmy, had made him forgetful or careless; so they did not notice the front door opening and a lady with her arm in a sling coming out.

"Young men, young men!" she shouted, walking down the path towards them.

"Quick run," said David, "she'll only want us to do jobs." And with that he was off. Timmy was not so quick and as she was now at the garden gate he thought it would be rather rude to run off. Anyway, jobs could mean money, and with enough money, he might be able to buy the traps.

"Will you go to the shop for me, because as you can see, I have broken my arm." she said.

"OK" said Timmy, though he wondered why she could not go to the shop herself, even with a broken arm. He followed her into the house while she sorted out the money.

"I'll give you some apples for your family, when you get back" She said. "Thanks." said Timmy, though what he really wanted was money, not apples. "If you go through that door, and open the first box you see," she said, "take one apple out. That's to be going on with, while you're walking to the shop." Timmy slid back the lid on the big wooden box and poked his head over the top. A wonderful sweet smell hit him; he had never smelled apples like this before, it really made his mouth water. She told him they were Russets, and they were as good as they smelled he thought, as he munched away while skipping along the lane to the shop.

The lady only wanted five items, one of which was a packet of tea, but try as he might, Jimmy could not remember the tea. He knew he was one item short and it was a packet of something or other. The shopkeeper tried to help him, suggesting all sorts of things, but it was no good, his mind refused to work. In the end Timmy settled for a packet of salt, convincing himself that salt really was what she wanted. But of course it wasn't and Timmy soon found himself going back to the shop to change it. He was feeling down in the dumps now, and there wasn't much skipping in his steps as he trudged along the now familiar lane.

When he got near the village centre, he could heard a bit of a commotion, and going round a corner, found his friends playing football in the street. So of course he joined in, playing in goal, all thoughts of shopping forgotten, until one of the footballers said "I'm going home for tea."

"Tea" shouted Timmy. "Tea! I should be going to the shop to get a packet of tea." With that he picked up his coat and tore off to the shop, but it was too late, the shop had closed.

"What shall I do now?" puffed Timmy, as he sat on

the shop window ledge, trying to get his breath back. "I know, I'll go and see Mum, she might be able to help."

"Well young man" said his mother, after Timmy had explained his predicament. "Nearly all the problems and the scrapes you get into are of your own making. You do know that, don't you?"

"Yes, I do know that Mum. But can you help me?" whined Timmy. "Please Mum."

Hiding a half smile she said sternly. "You're lucky Timmy, I have an unopened packet, it's probably not the right brand, but if Mrs Bush has completely run out of tea it'll be better than nothing, and you'll have to get me a new packet first thing in the morning."

So once again, he set off on his weary way down the lane. His legs were getting quite tired by now.

Mrs Bush was waiting for him by the gate. He now knew her name, having been informed by his mother.

"I didn't think you were coming back" she said. Timmy didn't say anything, as he handed over the packet of tea. "Well that's not my normal brand," she said. "I normally have Lyons, the shopkeeper knows that."

"He didn't have any" lied Timmy, "So I got you the Dividend tea. My Mum buys that so it must be good, and if you don't collect the stamps, can I take the one on the packet home?" The lady smiled and told him to follow her into the house. She let him sort through the straw to find the six biggest apples and put them in a paper bag for him.

"What about the stamp?" asked Timmy.

"OK," she laughed as she cut the stamp off the tea packet. "Your Mother must be proud of you young man."

I don't think so, thought Timmy as he put the stamp in his back pocket and headed off for home. David was sitting on the farm gate with his younger sister when Timmy passed.

"What did you have to do for her, then Timmy?" he asked.

"I went to the shop for her and she gave me these apples to take home." said Timmy.

"You went all the way to the shop and back for a few crummy apples?" laughed David, "that's over two miles."

"Well actually" said Timmy sheepishly, "I went twice, because I forgot what I wanted the first time." David nearly fell off the gate with laughter, and with tears in his eyes said, "You and your mate Tom think you are so clever but really you're quite stupid. We've got apples and you could have had for them for nothing, in fact if you want some more Sis will go and get you some."

"I wouldn't mind a few more," said Timmy.

"OK," said David turning to his sister. "Jane go and get him some from the store. Mum won't see you; she's still helping Dad with the cows." She came back with an armful, and Timmy put them in his jerkin. Jerkins were good coats, because they were tight around the waist. All sorts of things could be put in them, leaving your hands free. So off he went doubly happy, munching away on his extra apples, carrying the family apples in the bag.

On his many trips along this now very familiar lane, Timmy had noticed a lot of primroses growing on a bank on the far side of a big ditch. He thought it would be nice if he picked a bunch for his mother. To get to the other side, he would have to go over a bridge and gate, into a field, then walk back along and squeeze though the hedge on the top of the bank. This he did, leaving the bag of apples on the field side of the hedge. He only had the apples in the bag, having eaten the ones in his jerkin. When he arrived on the top of the bank, having squeezed through the hedge, he found he was in the wrong place and had to work his way along to where the primroses were growing. This was not an easy task, as the bank was quite steep. The ditch was smelly and looked pretty deep. But he managed to gather a good bunch of primroses and feeling rather pleased with himself squeezed back through the hedge. His face was a picture of horror when he saw the cows. They were stood where he had left the apples. He ran towards them, fearing the worst. Yes, they had eaten the lot. One even had part of the brown paper bag hanging out of the side of its mouth. This soon disappeared the same way as the apples. There were tears of anger and frustration in his eyes as climbed over the gate. What a waste of a day, he thought. Little did he know it, there was worse to come.

"Are you sure you didn't eat those apples Timmy?" His mother said, eyeing him keenly.

"No Mum, I'm telling the truth, the cows did eat our apples."

"Well sit down and eat your tea." She said putting the primrose in a vase. "I'm not very hungry Mum." He said. This was not surprising, because he was full of apples. His mother turned to look at him closely.

"What's the matter with you?" she said, "You're always hungry. Are you ill?" Timmy did in fact feel a bit queasy. In fact he felt a bit sick. In fact he felt very sick and made a dash for the back door. He got the door open, but too late it was all over the door step. Of course it was all apples he brought up. His mother was furious. "So you did eat all the apples." She shouted at him.

"No Mum, they were different apples," wailed Timmy "The cows did eat our apples."

"Don't tell me any more lies and get to your room," she said crossly.

So he went to bed, with a bowl on the floor just in case there were more apples to come up. He was thoroughly dejected and miserable.

"If I hadn't picked those silly flowers this would not have happened." He groaned. "I shall never try to be nice again." But it wasn't long before he was asleep and the morning would bring another day.

"Things didn't seem to go all that well for Timmy, did they Granddad?" said Stuart. "Well no, but as his mother said, most of his seemingly bad luck was of his own making."

"Granddad" said James, "How could those boys make money from moles and did the traps kill the moles?"

"Yes the traps did kill the moles," said his grandfather "The pelts were sold to the fashion industry. They used them mainly for luxury linings in coats and waistcoats and things like that."

"I think that's cruel," said James with feeling. "Moles are nice little animals. I'm not sure that I like those boys so much now."

"You mustn't judge them too harshly," said his grandfather. "I don't think people were so squeamish in those days, I certainly can't remember there being any animal rights movements, or any organisations like them. What you must remember is, moles can be a nuisance and farmers do not want them in their fields. If there are other people willing to pay for the animals, or there skins, then it is a normal supply and demand situation. As for Timmy, he would not have even thought about it being cruel, or otherwise. Living in the country, he wouldn't see any difference between catching moles and catching wild rabbits. In Timmy's household they had rabbit for the main meal at least once a week. Rabbits were almost a staple diet in those austere, post-war years."

"Did Timmy ever get enough money to buy the traps Granddad?" said Stuart.

"Timmy enlisted the help of Tom and together they eventually raised enough money to pay for half the traps," said his grandfather. "They had come to an agreement with David, to pay the other half from the proceeds of the pelts. The enterprise was not a great success and ended in a minor catastrophe."

With their new collection of traps, Tom and Timmy went to see a farmer that Timmy knew well. "You can go moling in my fields if you like, young Timmy" He said. "But you ain't going to get many, cause the ground is frosty and hard. You'll have to wait 'til 'tis a bit warmer." So it was a few weeks later before the trapping partnership could start their operations.

In the beginning all went well. They pretended they were trappers in the Canadian Rockies. This just goes to show how much imagination they had, because most of their trapping was on the flat moors and levels. When they had trapped a dozen or more, the pelts were bundled up and mailed to a firm up in Bristol. This company was very efficient and by the return of post, the boys would receive there remuneration plus a refund on the cost of postage.

To start with the boys were very keen. It did not take them long to pay off David and they were soon making a profit. However the enthusiasm did not last because they had to go further and further afield to set their traps. Generally speaking they would only go out when money was required for some specific reason, or item. One Thursday evening the traps were set with the intention of collecting them on Friday. But there was a deluge of rain on Friday, it was as if the heavens had opened, so the traps could not be collected. On Saturday morning both Tom and Timmy were grounded for some misdemeanour, or something they had done, or not done, as the case may be. They didn't mind too much, because of the excitement generated by a football match that was going to take place in the afternoon. Almost the whole population of the village, (or so it seemed to Timmy) were going to the local town to watch the village football team play in a cup final. Tom, Timmy and friends were keen supporters of the team and watched all home matches. If there was enough room in the team's transport, they were quite often taken to away matches. From the touchline, they screamed and shouted their support for the team, whom they called the Ragged A---- Rover's. Their raucous chanting and singing, plus the nickname, gave opposing teams and supporters a lot of amusement and eventually became the unofficial name for their team. Sunday was a big day as well, because it was a village bus trip to Weymouth. Tom and Timmy loved this annual outing, which was organised by the Royal British Legion, and Weymouth was their favourite seaside town, with its good beach and interesting harbour. All these activities and excursions meant the traps could not be collected until Monday and it would have to be in the evening, when school had finished.

As they neared the field where the traps had been set, Tom shouted, "Oh No!" Timmy turned to look at him, noticing the look of dismay on his face.

"Whatever is the matter with you?"

"Look there are cows in the field, I bet we've lost a lot of our traps." Tom said as they raced towards the field. And indeed they had, only two could be found. Whenever a farmer gave permission to trap in his fields the boys always ascertained the likelihood of cows being put in them. They had done so, on this occasion, but of course that was five days ago. The farmer would not have known they still had the traps down and had moved the cattle on Saturday.

"I suppose that's the end of our trapping enterprise."

said Tom as they trudged home. "I don't care though; I was getting fed up with mole trapping anyway."

"So was I." agreed Timmy. Though in reality it was not so much Timmy was getting fed up with trapping, it was more to do with his thoughts on killing so many moles. When they had started he was as enthusiastic as Tom, especially when they were making a lot of money. But now he was beginning to feel differently. He had not wanted to say anything to Tom, ashamed of his feelings. He was afraid Tom would laugh at him and say he was squeamish. It was many years later that Timmy broached the subject with Tom and Tom did laugh, just as he expected he would, but then unexpectedly Tom had said. "I was not very happy about trapping right from the start, but I did not want to say anything to you in case you took the Mickey."

Timmy hung the two remaining traps in his father's garden shed, there they remained for many years and might well be there to this day.

"Granddad," said Stuart, "I don't understand how they lost their traps. You said there were cows in the field. But what difference did that make?"

"I should have explained it better," said his grandfather. "The traps were put in mole runs or tunnels. Very little of these devices were visible above ground and because they were rusty and earth coloured, almost impossible to find in a big field. To counteract this, Tom and Timmy put markers by each trap. The markers were sticks of about three or four feet in length and painted white. They did not want cows in the field, because the cows would knock down the markers and make the traps hard to find. On this particular day they had forgotten the markers and so had to cut fresh sticks out of the hedges. They had done this before, when the markers had been forgotten the foliage was left on the sticks to make them more visible. The boys couldn't remember what type of bush or tree they had used for markers, whatever sort they were the cows must have found them delicious, because they had eaten the lot, making it very difficult to find the traps."

"Timmy doesn't seem to have much luck with cows does he Granddad?" said Stuart.

"Well I'm glad they lost their traps," said James, "because I still think it's cruel."

"So do I." said Stuart as they all trudged home for their tea.

The Wrath of Mrs Vicar

The car drew up outside their house and out tumbled the grandchildren. They bounded down the long path and almost knocked their grandmother over with their enthusiastic hugs. James and Stuart were certainly getting big and they were very boisterous, so much so that Mary wondered how her parents were going to handle them all day. Especially in the evening because she was picking them up quite late; her parent's television could only receive three channels and there was not even a video player or a computer in the house. She gave the boys a carrier bag containing comics and magazines.

"They're for this evening in case there is nothing on the television," she said.

"Thanks Mum, but we won't need these," laughed James," because granddad's going to tell us a story, he promised. Didn't you granddad?" "Well I did sort of," said John. "It's a good job I've thought of a few narratives I think you'll like." And so it was after tea they settled down and he told them the following tales.

"Timmy, Timmy come down here at once!" shouted Timmy's mother. Timmy opened his bedroom door.

"Did you call Mum?" he asked; he had of course heard her, but he was stalling for time. Timmy had heard the knock on the front door and had heard his mother talking to someone and he had good idea who that someone was.

"Yes I did; come down here," her voice sounded as if

she was really angry. With a sense of dread, Timmy slunk down the stairs and there, just as he knew she would be, was the vicar's wife and Mrs Vicar did not look very happy at all. Tom and Timmy called her Mrs Vicar because they did not know the Vicar's surname, so if she was the vicar's wife, she must be Mrs Vicar.

It had all started innocently enough. Timmy had been flying his kite; this was no ordinary kite, being big and yellow, with an aluminium frame. It had been given to him by an uncle, who had told him it was an RAF target kite. Timmy didn't know what this meant, he had never heard of a target kite, all he did know was that it was the best flying kite he had ever had. Tom, who was a great model plane maker and flyer, had helped Timmy get the kite off the ground and was suitably impressed with his friend's new acquisition; once off the ground it did not seem to need any assistance from the operator,

"It's as if it is flying itself," cried Timmy with delight,

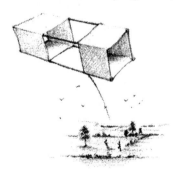 as he unwound the big ball of twine that had come with the kite; he had never seen a kite fly so high.

"I'll get some of my father's seafishing lines," said Tom. "Then we will really see how high it'll fly."

Reel after reel of seafishing line was added, this fishing line was strong but light and the kite got higher and higher, until it was not much more than a big dot in the sky. This probably was not a good idea, as this part of Somerset was a low flying area for the new jet fighters based at the nearby airfield.

The kite seemed to be dropping a bit and was not above them in the big field as it had been to start with, it was now well out over the village; so at a leisurely rate they had begun to wind it in.

"I think the wind might be dropping," said Tom as he wound the fishing line back onto the reels. The winding got quicker and quicker as the kite got lower and lower on the horizon, but it did not seem quick enough. Soon Timmy was hauling the line in, hand over hand and it wasn't long before there was more fishing line on the ground than on the reels because Tom could not keep up. Still the kite descended; that would have been OK if the kite had been descending on the field, but there was still so much line out it was a long way away and at the present rate of descent would come down on the other side of the houses. Timmy picked the line up and ran across the field. This seemed to keep the kite in the air for a while, but when he got to the hedge at the end of the field and could go no further the kite dropped like a stone; out of sight and behind the houses just as they had feared. Tom was doing his best to wind up the fishing line that was now in a heap on the ground, except for the bit that was across the field, where Timmy had run with it to try to keep the kite in the air. Timmy was almost jumping up and down in anguish as Tom tried to sort out the knots in the fishing line that was lying in a muddle on the ground.

"You've got to leave that!" he cried. "Let's go and find my kite."

"I can't leave it," said Tom. "My dad will kill me if I don't return all his fishing lines. He probably will anyway if he finds out I have been using them to fly a kite; so if you give me a hand to untangle this lot, we can go and find your kite." With growing frustration Timmy helped with the untangling, which was not as bad as it first looked. The line was soon unravelled and Tom was winding it in as they crossed the field; but it was only as far as the hedge where the line went over the top of the telephone wires. No amount of pulling would retrieve any more line.

"The kite must be stuck on something," said Timmy. "If we cut it off here, then go and find the kite, we can pull the line in from the other end." Tom thought about this suggestion, but instead of cutting the line he started to unwind the reel, looking for a knot where he had joined the lines together. Timmy was almost jumping up and down in frustration at this delay and was off down the road following the line overhead, long before Tom had found a knot and undone it.

"What are you doing then Young Timmy?" said an elderly man in his garden as Timmy went by, staring upwards intently trying to follow the fishing line.

"I'm following a line," said Timmy, "my kite's on the end of it." The man looked up, following Timmy's gaze: he did not know what sort of line Timmy was talking about and his eyes were not that good so he could not see the fishing line.

"That's a strange lad, Mary." he said to his wife as he watched Timmy go down the road, with his head back staring up into the sky. A few minutes later along came Tom, acting in the same manner.

"What's the matter with these kids; am I going mad or are they?" he said shaking his head.

"I don't know Jim," she said, "but those two are always up to something so it's probably best we if don't know."

The line went over houses, electric wires and trees. At last Timmy found it in Church Lane; hanging just over the top of the Vicarage wall. The wall was about ten feet tall and smooth. 'Well, I can't climb that', thought Timmy and there was nothing to hand he could use to pull it down. He was joined by Tom and even standing on Tom's shoulders he was a long way short of reaching the kite.

"I wonder if I can climb the wall from the other side?" mused Timmy.

"You might," said Tom. "You can get into the Vicarage garden, by going through the school playground and there might be something there to help you climb this big wall." So Timmy went back down the lane and over the school wall, which was about five feet high. He crossed the playground, over another wall, through a small orchard, climbed over a small gate and found himself in the Vicarage Garden. Timmy could see where the fishing line crossed the big wall and there would be no problem climbing up from this side. Against the wall grew a large tree, whose branches had been trained along the wall on what looked to Timmy like wires. The kite was towards the end of the wall and the last three branches on this side of the tree finished just under the kite.

"That's great," said Timmy to himself. "It would not be any easier to get up that wall if I had a ladder." Timmy was halfway up when his attention was taken by what appeared to be fruit hanging from the branches. They were rather like large plums, though in appearance looked more like apples. He picked one and was rather surprised to find  the skin was furry and soft; it smelt rather sweet, so tentatively he bit into it and was surprised by the taste. It was beautiful, sweet and juicy.

'I don't know what they are,' thought Timmy as he

picked a few more and put them in his pockets, 'they are blooming nice though'. The juice was running down his chin as he climbed on to the top branch. Looking over the top of the wall he dropped a fruit down for Tom to taste; who promptly declared. "They're peaches Timmy."

"Peaches?" said Timmy. "Are you sure? I've only had peaches out of a tin. I thought peaches were a foreign fruit, I certainly didn't know they grew on trees in this country." Timmy was just about to climb onto the top of the wall when the wire which was holding the branch in place came away from the wall. Timmy hung on to the top of the wall by his fingertips, but not for long, they soon gave out and he fell to the next branch below. The weight of him falling pulled the supporting wire out of the wall on this branch also; so he fell to the third and last one, with the same consequences.

"Are you hurt?" shouted Tom.

"No, I don't think so." replied Timmy, though he was a bit shaken.

"I'll come round," shouted Tom. He found Timmy nursing a cut knee where it had scraped down the wall.

"We'll soon fix that," said Tom as he tied a handkerchief around Timmy's leg to stem the blood. Looking up at the wall he said, "You certainly made a mess of that tree though." All three branches were now hanging down; even the top one was almost touching the ground. They filled their pockets with fruit; climbed up the main trunk of the tree and on to the top of the wall. The kite was just being lowered to the floor when the Vicar came through the church gates and into the lane. His intention was to go into the Vicarage, but when he saw Tom and Timmy he walked down towards them.

"What are you two boys doing up there?" he said, his neck straining back as he looked up towards them sitting on the wall.

41

"We're just rescuing our kite," said Tom.

"What's it doing up there?" replied the Vicar.

"It landed up here," came the reply from Tom. He put his hand over his mouth and said quietly to Timmy, "For a man with God on his side, he doesn't seem very bright, does he?" Timmy burst out laughing, so much so, Tom had to hang on to him, because he thought Timmy was going to fall off the wall.

"I don't know what you find so funny, young man." said the Vicar, turning a little pink. "You can both get off my wall and come down here at once."

With Tom lying on top of the wall and leaning over as far as he could; he helped Timmy get down off the wall, because Timmy's leg was now quite stiff from the graze he had received from the fall. Timmy held on to Tom's hand and slid down the wall, but even with Tom's help there was still a long drop to the ground. Timmy landed OK, but the whole operation was not helped at all by his inability to stop giggling. Now it was Tom's turn. He climbed over the edge and hung on to the top by his fingertips; straining up Timmy could now just reach Tom's feet.

"OK," he shouted, "let go Tom." Tom did just that and they both landed in a heap at the Vicar's feet. Even lying on the ground, Timmy was unable to contain his mirth; the more he tried to suppress the laughter, the worse it got. So much so, his side was now hurting and there were tears in his eyes. This uncontrollable giggling was of course infectious and it wasn't long before Tom was in the same state as Timmy. The Vicar was now getting quite perplexed and his face was reddening as his anger grew. He was a big man and had been some sort of hero in the war; he was not used to this sort of behaviour and did not quite know how to deal with it. His war record and his status as a clergyman meant that he was given, and expected a lot of respect; even by those not of his flock. He ordered the boys to stop laughing and get up off the ground. They stood up OK, but try as they might, they could not stop giggling. The Vicar was now looking very angry and was probably thinking very ungodly thoughts. Tom even thought he was going to hit him and was getting ready to duck. Instead the Vicar turned abruptly and walked back towards the vicarage; but as he opened the door he turned back to look at the boys and said, "Don't forget I know who you are."

With the Vicar gone, Timmy pulled in the fishing line and Tom wound it on the big fishing reels. They did this as quickly as they could, because the Vicar might go into his garden and see how they had messed up his tree. By the time they had reached Timmy's house, the pair of them had stopped laughing; they were now worried about the tree.

"It's unlikely he will see it tonight," said Timmy. "It's now almost dark, so I shouldn't think he, or anyone else will be going into the garden."

"I've got the beginning of a thought," said Tom, his face wrinkled in concentration. "Tomorrow is Sunday isn't it?"

"Yes, so what?" said Timmy, a little mystified.

"Well" said Tom, "I bet everyone in that household goes to the early morning service."

"I bet they do." replied Timmy with a huge smile; as he realised Tom's train of thought. "We might be able to peg those branches back up, or do something to make it look a bit better. What time does the service start?"

"I don't know?" said Tom. "But it will be on the church notice board." They went back down the church lane, crept passed the vicarage, ready to run if the vicar or anyone else came out and obtained the information they required from the notice board. Once again the two were standing outside Timmy's house; this time making arrangements for the morning. The plan was to get up early and wait for the service to begin. In theory the village would be quite, early morning risers would be in church; so if things went wrong no one would see them.

"I don't know how we're going to reach the top branches Tom?" said Timmy.

"I do," said Tom. "We've got to go through the school playground, so we will borrow the ladder that's in the school shed."

The morning was bright and the plan was being executed to perfection. Although Tom's theory of all early morning risers going to church was doubtful, they arrived at the school without being seen and had climbed over the wall into the playground, located the ladder and set off for the Vicarage. The ladder was on Tom's shoulder when they arrived at the

 Vicarage garden armed with a hammer, nails and a ball of string. All was going well, probably too well, because catastrophe was about to strike. They were passing the greenhouse when Timmy spotted something red inside.

"Look Tom, there's ripe tomatoes in the greenhouse." he said. Tom turned to look and the ladder on his shoulder turned as well, with disastrous consequences. Not just one, but two panes of glass smashed onto the floor. They looked at each other aghast. Why did everything have to go wrong?

"If we clear up all the broken glass and take out all the bits that are left in the frames," said Timmy, "you might not be able to tell the glass is missing."

"It might work," said Tom. "At least it might fool them for a while." So they set about clearing all the broken glass, putting the bits in a sack they had found; but before they could start pulling out the bits of glass which were left in the frames, an upstairs window in the Vicarage was thrown open. They thought it was Mrs Vicar, though were not quite sure as the house was some distance from the greenhouse. When she shouted, "What are you two boys doing down there?" It was obvious to both of them it was Mrs Vicar, so they dropped everything and ran. Puffing and panting they arrived back at the front gate to Timmy's house and stopped to catch their breath.

"Do you think she recognised us?" Gasped Timmy.

"The house was a long way off so maybe she didn't." panted Tom. "It's about time we had a bit of luck. Anyway I'm going to creep back into my house and go back to bed; no one will be up yet and they will think I have been in bed all the time."

"That's a good idea," said Timmy. "I shall do the same."

Timmy stole into his house as quietly as possible, holding his breath when the kitchen door creaked and the cat meowed. He took the fruit out of his jacket pockets and put them on the sideboard; peaches from the escapade of the night before and tomatoes that were freshly picked. His plan was to hide them in his room and then when the coast was clear he would eat them at his leisure. As he hung his coat up he heard movement from one of the bedrooms upstairs; someone was getting up. He made a dash for the stairs; making sure he missed the two steps that creaked, he reached the top and fled along the landing. Opening his bedroom door as quietly as possible he slipped inside. Timmy was only just in time because as he stood with his back to the door, breathless and almost shaking with the exploits of the morning; he heard a door open and someone went into the bathroom. He climbed into bed and listened to the movement and noises as the rest of the household got up. It was then, with a despairing dread, he heard the loud rat-a-tat-tat, on the front door and his mother calling him. He went down the stairs, barefooted and pulling on his trousers, hoping to show he had not been outside that morning and had only just got up. This charade might well have succeeded, if his mouth had not dropped open, as spotted he something behind Mrs Vicar. His mother was saying with some relief in her voice, as he came down the stairs.

"Well it was not my boy this time because he has been in bed all night and has only just got up as you can..." she stopped mid-sentence as she saw the dismayed look on Timmy's face and followed his almost mesmerised gaze. There on the sideboard, looking for all the world like trophies for sport or some other achievement, were two neat rows of peaches and tomatoes.

"What are those Timmy?" said his mother, her voice going very deep as Timmy slowly tried to back up the stairs. But it was no good; the game was up. Tom and Timmy had laughed at the vicar, but Mrs Vicar was a different kettle of fish altogether, although she was not very big she was a formidable and intimidating woman; the retributions were terrible. When Tom and Timmy met the next day to go to school, they thought the worst was over, but they had reckoned without Miss Madwit, the headmistress. She made them stand in front of the whole school.

"Look at these two boys children and tell me what you see? I'll tell you what you see," she said without waiting for an answer. "You see two thieves."

"But Miss –" started Timmy.

"No buts Timothy," she interrupted him. "You are thieves and worse. Did you or did you not steal the Vicar's peaches?"

46

"Yes Miss," they answered in unison.

"Did you steal the tomatoes?"

"Yes Miss," they answered the same way.

"Did you steal the School ladder?"

"No Miss, we only borro –" But she cut Tom off before he could finish.

"It's not borrowing to take things without permission. Did you have permission?"

"No Miss," they said, now thoroughly dejected.

"No," she said. "So that was stealing wasn't it?"

"Yes Miss," They answered, once again in unison. Miss Madwit was really getting into her stride now.

"Did you break down the tree?" she demanded.

"Yes Miss."

"Did you smash two panes of glass in the greenhouse?"

"Yes Miss."

"Were you trespassing in both the Vicarage garden and the school playground?"

"Yes Miss."

"You two boys are a disgrace to the school and your families and if you don't mend your ways soon, may God help you, because if God doesn't help you, I do not know anyone who will. You have let yourselves and everyone else down and you people..." she turned to look at the assembled children; "must not talk to them at all today, even at playtime. Not that playtime will be much of a problem." She turned back and pointed a shaking finger at the wretched twosome. "Because you two are not going to have any playtime today or for the next week. Now go to your seats and sit down, I don't want to hear anther word from either of you for a long time."

It was a quiet and disconsolate pair that left the school that evening; heading for home with hardly a word spoken between them. They were almost home when Timmy stopped walking and turned to look at his friend.

"Are we really very bad Tom?" he enquired.

"No," said Tom. "No we're not bad, we're just unlucky." Timmy thought about this.

"Yeah," he said as he started to walk home again. "Yeah, you're probably right, we're just unlucky. What are you doing after tea?"

"Well I thought we might go and mooch around that old house on the moor; it's been empty for weeks."

"Yes that's a good idea Tom; see you after tea then."

Goats

"Those boys certainly got themselves into a lot of scrapes, Granddad," said James, "Do you think they were bad?"

"No, I don't think they were bad," said the old man. "Just a bit unlucky as Tom often said, but as it has been said many times before; they brought most of their problems onto themselves."

"What I want to know, Granddad," said James. "is what were the terrible retributions they suffered?"

"Well, to start with they had to work all day in the Vicarage garden, which was a bit of a bind, because they had planned to go fishing. The next few weekends found them working in the garden as well; but it was not too bad because as well as the peaches and tomatoes, there were blackcurrants, redcurrants, gooseberries, raspberries and a whole host of other things. Anyway, they did not carry out the full sentence, because they were deemed more trouble than they were worth. Trouble seemed to follow them whatever they did. It wasn't Tom's fault he dropped the flower pots and broke them. It wasn't Timmy's fault he forgot to turn off the hosepipe and there was a flood. But it was Tom's fault he let in the goats. He thought they would eat all the weeds and save him a job. They did of course, along with everything else.

"Where did the goats come from, Granddad?" asked James.

"Ah well, that's another story," said the grandfather.

At the bottom of the village were the cider works, and

at certain times of the year burnt sugar would be used in the process. What it was used for the boys did not know, it had been suggested it was for colouring, if that is so it was certainly extravagant because at that time sugar was severely rationed, as were sweets. All they knew was that an old man who worked there, a grandfather of one of their friends, would sometimes give them big lumps of it, wrapped in newspaper. For Timmy it was the best thing he had ever tasted and when they were using this process he would go there every morning before school. He would hang about until the last minute before chasing off to school and sometimes he got his reward. He had lots of friends on the days he arrived at school with lumps of burnt sugar. In fact, some would be waiting for him at the crossroads just before the school. On this particular day there were three of them, Tom, Timmy and Mick, the old

man was Mick's grandfather.

They had been told there was no sugar today and as there was plenty of time before school, were amusing themselves by teasing the goats. In the field or yard next to the works, scattered about and all higgledy-pickledy were lots of cider barrels. Among these barrels lived several goats. One of the boys would get the goats to chase him and then jump into a barrel. The goats would then headbutt the barrel to try and get at the occupant. This was a bit dodgy because the goats were quite strong and vicious and the barrels were in various states of decay. The only way the person in the barrel could get away was for someone else to get the goats attention, usually by throwing lumps of mud at them and then that person would jump in a barrel of his own. In this way they went all over the field leaving it later and later before jumping into a barrel. The boys got tired before the goats, so they decided to work their way back to the gate. They were almost back to where they had started when Timmy thought he could make it to the gate. He almost got caught and had to make a huge jump into the last barrel, to his dismay it was about three quarters full of water. By the time the other boys had got the goats attention and he could get out he knew it was not water, it was cider, very old cider and it stank. Timmy felt really miserable; he was soaking wet and smelly. What would his mother say? And not only that, he would be late for school. What would Miss Madwit say?

"I've got an idea," said Tom. "Why don't you jump into the river? It will wash out all that stinking cider and you can tell your Mum you fell in the river." This is what he did, just as Miss Miggs the infant teacher was cycling by. This was really bad luck because she lived in a different direction and did not normally pass this way. She was quite surprised to see Timmy jump in the river with all his clothes on, especially as it was a cold, overcast morning. By the time Timmy got home he was freezing. His mother took one look at him, stripped off his wet clothes and gave him a good rubbing down with a towel. He was then put to bed with a hot water bottle and loads of blankets, but Timmy could not stop shivering even when extra heating was put in the room. He did feel strange and by the time the doctor arrived, he was quite feverish. One minute he was sweating, the next he was shivering. There was talk about hospitalisation, but it was decided he could stay home with the district nurse calling early in the mornings and the doctor in the afternoons. It was a long time before the fever broke and it left Timmy very tired and sorry for himself, but he was soon to make a full recovery. He was feeling much stronger and sitting up in bed, when his mother confronted him with her knowledge that he had not fallen in the river but had jumped.

"Did you do it just to show off Timmy?" she said.

"But it wasn't like that Mum," cried Timmy. "I jumped in a barrel of old smelly cider. I didn't know it was in there, so then I jumped in the river to wash it off."

"Oh Timmy, what am I to do with you?" said his mother, as she put her arm around his thin shoulders and gave him a squeeze. "The way you carry on, I don't think you'll make it to adulthood." She whispered, a tear in her eye.

"But he did make it didn't he, Granddad?" asked James. "Oh yes," laughed his grandfather. "He made it OK though it was touch and go sometimes, but in those early days he was resilient and was soon out and about again with his great friend Tom. It wasn't too long before they were into their next adventure."

The Ghosts of Orchard House

"What was the next adventure after Timmy got better then, Granddad?" said Stuart

"Well you might not like this one," said the old man. "In some parts it's rather grotesque."

They had been planning it for weeks and tonight the scheme was to be put into operation.

"It is a brilliant plan and can't go wrong; it's just so simple." said Tom. He and Timmy were in their den, which was a shed in Timmy's garden. From this shed they planned most of their activities and this afternoon was no exception; they were making final arrangements for the evening's exploit.

Every few weeks a man would come to the village, to give a film show in the British Legion Hall. Tom and Timmy's families were keen patrons, as were most of the villagers. The hall was about three quarters of a mile away and the two boys usually walked up through the village, with their respective families. Whoever arrived first would wait outside for the other to turn up; they would then go inside and sit together with the other children from the village. This gang of children were sometimes quite noisy and were often told to be quiet. Although Tom and Timmy liked the films, especially the comedies with their laughter being the loudest in the hall; tonight they were giving the film show a miss. They were instead, going on a secret mission; at least it was a secret to their parents and all other adults. Their mission was to prove to the others in the gang that the big empty house on the hill was not haunted and they were not frightened of ghosts. There had always been talk of the house being haunted; especially now as the house had been empty for a long, long time. Tom and Timmy had scoffed at this idea and had laughed and teased the others, saying they were sissies and soft in the head to believe in such rubbish.

"Anyway," said Timmy. "I don't believe in ghosts and if there are such things as ghosts, I would like to meet one of them."

"Well I bet you two big heads would not stay in that house overnight," said David, one of the others in the gang. He had not liked being called a sissy and soft in the head.

"It wouldn't worry me," said Tom. "But my dad wouldn't let me stay out all night."

"I couldn't stay out all night either," said Timmy. "I could if it was the middle of the summer and we were going camping or something like that; but I wouldn't get away with it this time of the year."

"There you are," said David. "You two are all mouth, when it comes down to it, you're both chicken." He ran around flapping his arms and clucking like a hen. The others laughed and joined in the mocking of the Two T's. Tom was stung by the derision of his peers, he was not used to having the Mickey taken out of him and he was not going to stand for it. But it was Timmy who saved the situation with an inspirational idea.

"We could stay in that house for quite a long time on a Saturday night, Tom."

"How and why a Saturday night?" said Tom.

"We could on a film night," he said. "We could stay there until at least ten thirty, that is, if we didn't go to the show."

"What do you think about that then?" said Tom to the others; who having tired of running around and clucking like chickens, were now hooting and pretending to be ghosts instead. And so a compromise had been agreed; the big day had arrived and they were making their final preparations.

"Mum!" said Timmy after tea. "I want to go and see David, before the film show, we are swapping some foreign stamps."

"Yes that's OK, Timmy," she said. "But why do you ask? You normally just go out."

"Well I might arrive at the hall a bit later than you; so can I have the entrance money now please." She looked in her purse, but shook her head.

"Sorry, Timmy," she said. "I haven't got any change, but that's all right, I will pay for you even if you're not there, the lady on the door will remember."

"Darn!" said Timmy to himself as he walked up the road to meet Tom. He would have liked to have gone to see the films, but as he couldn't, he would have liked to have the entrance money instead. Now he was not going to get either and the money was to be wasted on an unused ticket.

"How are you going to get in the house and if you do manage to get in, how will we know that you are in there?" David had said, ever the sceptic.

"That's not a problem about getting in," said Tom. "Timmy and I can get in OK." They had been in the house several times in the past; gaining access through a coal chute. The chute led into the cellars and what wonderful cellars they were. Timmy thought they were fantastic, lots of brick arches and brick vaulted ceilings.

"They're just like the cellars in some of the scary films we've seen." he had said in awe, when he and Tom first saw the cellars in torchlight. They had found the coalbunker door by accident when Tom, trying to look through a window, had fallen into the brambles below. While trying to extradite himself, he had noticed a large hatch-like door slightly raised from the ground. He could raise it a few inches, but that was all, because of the years of undergrowth and brambles growing over the top. It took the boys ages to clear all this greenery away and when they had at last managed to lift the hatch they were surprised at the lack of steps. Instead there was a steep ramp sloping down under the house

"I wonder what it's for?" said Tom. Timmy thought about it for a moment and then said, "I think it's for coal. My aunt who lives in London has got something similar; that's a coal cellar down there and she calls this a coal bunker." The boys did not explore any further that day, as they were not properly equipped, but the next day they were back at the bunker, bright and early. Armed with a rope and torch, they were now ready to explore. Stone steps led up from the cellars to an unlocked door, which opened out into the main hall. What they had seen of the house it was empty, even though they had explored the house several times, they had not yet got as far as the attic rooms. But tonight the attic rooms were where they were heading. Part of the plan was to place a candle in one of the small attic windows. Poking out above the trees of a small copse; the top of the house and one attic window could just be seen, from the British Legion Hall. This was the requirement of the disbelievers. It would prove the two adventurers were actually in the haunted house.

It was almost pitch black as Tom and Timmy tied the rope and slid down the coal chute. They had hoped to be in position before nightfall, but it was a wet, windy night and the darkness had come early that evening. Picking there way with a dim torch held by Tom, they crossed the cellar and up the stone stairs. The torch really was dim and even this meagre light wouldn't hold out much longer. They would have to hurry to get to the top the house and into the attic room, before it failed altogether. It was the only torch they could find with even a bit of life left in it, having scoured both households, without success. The lads had reasoned that once they had lit the candles there wouldn't be any use for a torch and they were quite right. They had brought lots of comics to read; this would help to wile away the several hours of boredom while the others were watching the film show. The intrepid duo arrived on the third floor in what they assumed were the attic rooms; they thought these were the attic rooms because the walls leaned in slightly. They found a room with a window facing in the right direction and Timmy lit one of the candles. Setting it in the windowsill, he looked out of the window and was quite surprised he could not see any lights. Turning to Tom he said, "Are you sure we're in the right room? Because I can't see the light outside the Legion Hall."

"Of course we are," said Tom going over to the window to check for himself. It was then a car went by on the road and they could see by the lights why the hall was not visible. They were not high enough, they could not see over the trees.

"There must be another room above," said Tom. "I thought we were at the top of the house." With fading torch and by candlelight they searched unsuccessfully for another flight of stairs and were about to give up when Timmy opened what he thought was a cupboard door and discovered steps leading up. As he opened the door they both heard some sort of whooshing noise and a draft came down the stairs blowing out Timmy's candle. Timmy jumped back from the door.

"What was that?" he stuttered as he held onto Tom, not daring to take his eyes off the doorway that was now only illuminated by Tom's dim torch. Tom, who had been the more vocal of the two in their denunciations of ghosts, was now almost paralyzed with fear. Clinging together and shaking, they backed away from the door, which was now emitting an evil smell that seemed to come down the stairs and waft into the room. They backed out through the open door they had arrived in and onto the landing. Timmy, leaning forward pulled the door closed and then, helter-skelter, they ran down the stairs, through the cellars, up the coal chute, out into the gardens, not stopping there they ran down the drive and out onto the road. Sitting on a public seat near the gateway to the house, they tried to collect their breath and their thoughts.

"I've never been so frightened in all my life," said Timmy.

"Nor have I," said Tom with a great deal of feeling. But Tom was now beginning to recover his wits and was feeling rather ashamed of their headlong flight at the first show of something unusual.

"I still don't believe in ghosts," he said. "There could be any number of things that would make a noise like that." Timmy, who still had goose pimples all over his body, had sufficiently recovered to think about Tom's words.

"You could be right Tom," he said. "If you think about it, there was a really strong draft coming down the stairs. That could mean there is a window open or maybe broken in the attic room. It's stormy tonight and something could be blowing about in wind." They talked and discussed all the possibilities. This was done more to revive their shattered courage than anything else. With their courage partially restored they decided to return and have another go. Whereas before the flight down the stairs, they had pretended they were two intrepid explorers; now it was two timid little boys who crept back into the house. Jumping and starting at every little noise or rustle they crept back up the stairs and into the room with the awful smell. Timmy found the fallen candle and shielding it from the draft, relit it. Tom led the way with his now very dim torch, with Timmy just behind shielding the candle, they started up the stairs. The stairs seemed to be sticky and slimy and the smell was much stronger. Suddenly Tom ducked and fell back into Timmy, causing the candle to go out again.

"Something touched my face!" cried Tom. As Tom had fallen back the dim beam from his torch had shone straight up to the ceiling and Timmy had seen what it was.

 "It's OK, Tom," he almost shouted. "It's only a bat, look there's several of them." Once again they relit the candle and as it spluttered into life the sight that met their eyes was horrible. For many, many years the bats must have been roosting in this room, coming and going through the broken window. Clinging together on the stairs, Tom and Timmy were awe struck as they surveyed the nightmarish scene. This room was the only one in the house with any furniture. Well it might have been furniture once; they were not quite sure, because every surface was covered in a deep layer of bat droppings.

"How can a few bats like that make such a mess as

this?" whispered Tom.

"There's only a few here now," replied Timmy in an equally hushed voice. "Most of them are outside catching moths and insects; don't forget they hunt at night don't they? I bet this room is full of them in the day."

"Yeah, of course you're right, Timmy," he said, his whispered voice still had an incredulous sound to it. "There must be thousands of them when it gets daylight."

They backed down the stairs, finding it hard to keep their footing on the slippery steps, but not daring to touch anything to try and keep their balance. Once they were back in the room they had started from, Timmy shut the door to try and keep out the smell. They could shut out most of the smell but they could not shut out that nauseating scene from there minds.

"I can't stay in this house any longer, Tom," said Timmy. "Look, my hands are shaking and I don't feel well at all; I want a bath." This was quite a statement from a boy who would only wash when he was ordered and thought baths were for sissies and girls. Tom was glad that Timmy felt like that, he didn't want to stay in this house either. Timmy's hands were still shaking as he pulled himself up the coal chute and while trying to replace the cover, it slipped out of his hands, crashing to the ground with a loud bang that seemed to reverberate around the building. They heard footsteps coming up the drive and a man's voice said, "Who's there?" As the figure loomed up out of the darkness, the boys fled.

The following morning found Tom and Timmy being berated again by the gang.

"I knew you wouldn't go into that house last night," David jeered at them.

"We did go in and we can prove it," said Timmy. "There are a couple of candles and our comics in the house and if you come with us to collect them you will also see why we did not light the candle in the window. So the whole gang set out for the big house. They went via the copse, not wanting anyone to see them going up the drive. Leaving the rest in the copse Tom and Timmy took David and crept round the front of the house to the coal bunker. Pulling back the greenery Tom said, "Here you are, David; this is how we get in." He went to lift the lid up and to his astonishment found there was a padlock on it.

"Well, have you got the key?" said David.

"No," said Tom. "It's a new lock, it wasn't on there before." David looked at Tom and Timmy and shook his head.

"You two were not in this house last night and you have probably never been in it. So why don't you just admit it and stop all this malarkey?" Try as they might Tom and Timmy could not convince the others they had been in the house.

On Sunday afternoon, Tom and Timmy had to go to the Moravian Church Sunday school. This was a punishment for a recent misdemeanour and they still had another three weeks to go. The Moravian Church was quite close to the big empty house and the caretaker of the church and schoolroom also kept an eye on the empty house for a small remuneration. His wife helped in the church and took the Sunday school classes. She also helped with the film shows, taking the money and issuing tickets at the door. Tom and Timmy always thought she was a crafty old lady, but just how crafty they were about to find out. Before the class began she quite often had a general talk. Today she bought up the topics of comics and asked the children which ones they took, if any. Timmy volunteered he had the Eagle and Tom said the Dandy.

"Where were you two last night?" she said.

"We were at the films," they said almost together.

"Oh no you weren't, young men." she said. "Don't forget, I take the money and issue the tickets for the film show and you were not there last night. In fact young Timmy, I gave your mother back her money, because she had paid for you and you didn't turn up. I wonder if I had a look at the comics my husband found in the big house, I would find the Eagle and the Dandy?"

Oh what a predicament the Two T's were in. Here was the evidence to prove they had been in the big house; but if they admitted it they were in trouble."

"Well, you can't leave it there Granddad!" Shouted James. "Which did they choose?"

"Oh yes I can," said the grandfather, "Which would you have chosen?"

The Orangy Red Bike

"When did they get bikes Granddad?" asked Stuart. "You told us some time ago that they did eventually get them and terrorised the whole county. But they seemed to walk everywhere in the stories you have told us up till now."

"I don't think I said it quite like that," said the grandfather. "It was some time later they managed to get bikes of their own. You must remember this was the austere years after the Second World War and money was scarce in both their families, as it was in most of the families of their friends. Many, like Timmy's family had lost all their possessions when the cities were blitzed during the war. Also most things were rationed; Tom and Timmy had never known a time when rationing was not in operation. To them it was quite normal. "Tom and Timmy could both ride bikes but did not have bikes of their own. As with most of their friends, there were bikes in the family they could use, but these were normally big machines for adults, and generally speaking were ramshackle affairs. Tom had a new bicycle one Christmas; the acquisition of Timmy's bike turned into quite a saga.

Timmy was changing the wireless accumulator again. He was always very careful when doing this chore; because it would be more than his life was worth if he broke one of these essential bits of equipment. He would take the old one to the shop and collect the charged one. The village shop nearest to Timmy's house was really a collection of three wooden sheds. The smallest was on the right hand side of the lane, where wireless bits and pieces were held. It was also where accumulators were charged. The front of the main building was the general grocer's shop; this was connected to the rear shed which was really a work shop for bicycles, lawnmowers and other household equipment, though it did have a display window. Accumulator in hand, Timmy stared through this shop window again, his gaze riveted on the object of his desire. It was a boy's bicycle. Oh how he wished he could have that bike. He had looked at it longingly, ever since it had appeared in the window. At nights, he even dreamt of that bike, orangey red in colour, with a three speed and a saddle bag, it almost made his heart ache, he wanted it so much. Timmy knew his parents could not afford to buy the bike for him and he had not even asked, but when eating his tea that evening he said to his mother, "I've been looking at that bike again Mum, it is smashing. If I went apple picking with you, do you think I could earn enough money to buy it?"

"Well you could try, Timmy," she said. "Even if you don't make enough, you'll have some money for Christmas and that will make a difference."

And so he went apple picking, after school and at weekends. But apple picking is a boring job and to make matters worse, Timmy did not think he would ever make enough money. They were not eating apples that Timmy was picking and were not picked off the trees; they were for cider making and were picked up off the ground. Cider making was quite a big industry in this area and apple picking was a good additional source of income for the villagers in the run up to Christmas. Apples that did not fall off the trees naturally, were knocked off by the farmer or one of his workers, using a large pole. The pickers first picked the apples up in a bucket and when full transferred them into sacks. The sacks were stacked around the trunk of the trees and were picked up periodically by the farmer, who noted how many sacks were in each orchard. Each picker or groups of pickers, were allocated an orchard, or orchards and payment was per sack at the end of the season. Timmy soon found the pitfalls of apple picking. It was OK if you were picking up big apples like a variety called Morgan Sweets, a sack could be filled very quickly, but if they were of a small variety, it took ages. The apples he was picking at the moment were not too bad, they were called Tom Puds; the trouble was the grass was a bit long and there were a few stinging nettles. He had other problems as well. The orchard was the other end of the village, almost two miles away and even if he was on his mother's bike, it would take a long time. Especially as he would meet many of his friends on the way and of course, have to stop and have a chat. Sometimes he would not even reach the orchard. There were other things that took his time as well as chatting to his friends. One of these was the resurfacing of the lane that ran alongside the orchard. The orchard was higher than the road and from the fence he could look down on the activities. Timmy loved the smell of tar and the steamroller really fascinated him, especially when it broke a bridge. It was not really a bridge, just a pipe carrying a ditch that ran under the road. It might not have been much of a bridge but the steamroller was stuck fast, with the front roller down as far as the axle. The only other vehicle on site, at this time of the evening, was a grit lorry and this was unable to pull it out. It was dark by the time the steamroller had been rescued, with the assistance of two tractors from local farms and the lorry. Timmy of course had to stay to see the outcome and was starving by the time he got home. He had only picked two bags of apples all day.

With two weeks to go to Christmas, all the apples that the farmer required had been picked. It had been a glut year. He had easily fulfilled his contract to a large national cider company, who took away the unfermented apple juice in a tanker and he had more than enough for his own use and the few gallons he could sell from the farm. The men among the apple pickers had an arrangement with the farmer concerning any apples left over. He had agreed that they could pick the remaining apples and make their own cider, using his equipment. Timmy was seconded to this effort but as he would not be having any of the cider, the men said they would pay him the going rate per sack.

It was the Saturday before Christmas, when Timmy came storming home and flung himself down in a chair, his face red with anger.

"Whatever is the matter with you?" His mother said.

"Those men won't pay me my money, for the apples I picked." he almost shouted, tears in his eyes. "It's not my fault they lost their stupid cider."

"Oh dear, what have you been up to now, Timmy?" Said his mother, with a sense of foreboding, she feared the worst, because whenever he said, 'It wasn't my fault', it nearly always was. But for a change it was not Timmy's fault, in fact he did not have anything to do with it.

The men had decided Saturday would be the best day to start making the cider, as nearly all of them would be off work; apple picking was only a part time job for most of them. The farmer's cider making plant was a three story affair, similar to many in the area. An elevator was used to transport the apples from the collecting wagon to the top floor, where the crushing apparatus was housed. From here the crushed apples or pumice as it is called, is delivered to the press in the room below by means of a chute. A large wooden pallet is placed on the floor of the press, which is then covered with a piece of hessian. The hessian is about twice the size of the pallet and is placed on it diagonally so it overhangs the sides. A layer of apple pumice is then applied directly from the chute above and spread out almost to the edges; the overhanging Hessian is then turned over the top, forming a sort of envelope. Another pallet is added, and the process is repeated many times, making a multi layered sandwich. Traditionally straw was used instead of hessian. This pallet, hessian or straw and apple pumice sandwich (which is now called a cheese) is squeezed by a press. This particular press had one centre screw, many were double screws. The press is operated manually by a large lever or beam and the resulting apple juice is conveyed to the barrels or vats directly below via means of a chute, or a large flexible hose. In these large barrels or vats, the juice is left to ferment, thus forming cider.

The men had just finished the first pressing when they heard guffaws of laughter from below. It was the farmer and between fits of laughter he shouted, "Come down to the cellar."

The cellar was flooded and the farmer was paddling in what they thought was about three inches of water. Only it was not water it was apple juice and more of the precious stuff was pouring from the gaps in the barrel which had been allocated to them. The barrel had not been Plimed. As with a wooden boat; barrels will leak if allowed to dry out. Plim is probably a local name or terminology, meaning to swell the wood in barrels, making them water tight, or cider tight, and is normally achieved by using wet sacks or hessian. The only thing they could do was to rush upstairs and take the pressure off the press, but a lot of the precious liquid had been lost. It takes a long time to plim a barrel and there was not another available. There was a rather heated discussion to ascertain who was responsible. This was not helped one little bit by Timmy, who was laughing his head off, even more than the farmer, if that was possible.

"You shouldn't have laughed at them, Timmy," said his mother after she herself had stopped laughing. "Or certainly not in front of them; you're only a boy and should show a bit more respect for your elders. Though I do agree, you should be paid. I'll talk to your father, he'll get your money for you."

Timmy did get his money, but he was still a long way short of what was required for the bike.

"I'm going to see if Mr Gold will take a deposit on that bike, Mum." Said Timmy just a few days before Christmas.

"I wouldn't if I were you," said his mother. "How are you going to get the rest of the money?"

"I've still got the mistletoe to deliver," replied Timmy. While apple picking, he had noted the trees with mistletoe in them, and had already collected quite a lot.

"If you supplied every house in the village, Timmy, you still wouldn't have enough money." She replied.

"I know, Mum, but I'll see what he say's anyway." Timmy said as he went out of the door. His mother went to the window. She felt uneasy as she watched him, a lithe thin little figure skipping down the road towards the shop. She knew he would be back soon in a distraught state and she wouldn't be able to anything about it.

When Timmy got to the shop, he went round to the side window to have a last look at the bike. He could not believe his eyes. It was not there. In its place was a lawn mower. With his hands shaking, he cupped them over his eyes, trying to look into the back of the shop to see if it had been moved, but it was nowhere in sight. With his heart in his boots he rushed into the shop.

"I'm afraid it's been sold, young man," said the shopkeeper, ruffling Timmy's hair. Over the weeks he had watched Timmy staring at the bike, and knew he was trying hard to make enough money to buy it. He took hold of Timmy's shaking shoulders and knelt down in front of him. He was not noted as a kindly man, but could not help being a little moved by the tears welling in Timmy's eyes, the tremulous lips and the sheer look of devastation on his face.

"There will be other bikes, young man." He said not unkindly. "If you keep saving your money, I can promise you I can get more bikes as good, if not better than the red one you liked so much." But Timmy didn't want other bikes, the one he wanted was gone.

On his mother's insistence he delivered the mistletoe to the people who had placed an order with him. It was done with very little enthusiasm; the spring seemed to have gone out of his step. She really felt sorry for him, but what could she do?

By Christmas Timmy was back to his old self and was excited as ever, as he unwrapped the parcels, found at the bottom of his bed. There did not seem to be many presents and was he was soon unwrapping the last, which was quite large, rectangular and flat. Inside there was only a large piece of cardboard folded in half, written on the inside in large chalk letters was GO DOWNSTAIRS.

So he went down stairs and into the kitchen turning the light on, because it was still fairly dark. It was then he let out a shout.

"WOWEE, WOWEE!" he shouted, again and again. "WOWEE IT'S THE BIKE!" It was beautiful, even better than it looked in the shop window. He rushed upstairs and jumped on his parent's bed. If his shouting hadn't woken them, they were awake now with Timmy jumping up and down on their bed. There were actual real tears of joy in his eyes, all he could say was, "thank you, thank you, thank you," over and over again. When his mother had

calmed him down a bit she said, "You must thank your sisters as well, because they helped pay for it."

"OK," shouted Jimmy and he was halfway out the door before his mother stopped him.

"It's too early, Timmy, though I expect their awake now, with all the noise you've been making. Wait until they get up and then you can thank them properly."

"OK," said Timmy again, "but can I go out on the bike now, please."

"Of course you can," said his mother laughing, "But don't forget to get dressed first. If you look in the saddle bag, you will find a cape and leggings, because it will probably rain some time today. Your younger sister bought them."

Timmy was dressed and was pushing his bike out of the back door in about two minuets flat; he was of course going to see Tom. He didn't have to go to Tom's house because there was Tom on a brand new bike, waiting for him by the front gate.

Tom's bike was blue with drop handlebars and the newfangled type gears. They couldn't stop laughing as they raced around the village, visiting all their friends. It was almost lunchtime before Timmy remembered he was hungry and went home to have his breakfast.

"You're not jealous of Tom, with his brand new bike, are you Timmy?" His mother asked, as Timmy scraped the last crumbs off his plate.

"Of course I'm not, Mum," said Timmy with indignation. "I don't care what Tom, or anyone else has got, I've got the bike I wanted."

"It's the bestest bike in the world." He shouted as he ran out of the back door. She knew they wouldn't see him again until he was hungry, even though it was Christmas day. She put her hand on his father's shoulder as he sat at the table reading a paper.

"I know it was a bit of an effort, scraping the money together for that bike, but it's lovely to see him so happy and excited. Doesn't it make it all worthwhile?"

"Yes," said his father "It was a good present for him. But I wonder how well he'll maintain it and I bet it doesn't stay clean for long."

"Did Timmy keep his bike clean, Granddad?" said James.

"Oh yes," replied his grandfather. "Timmy loved that bike, it was always shiny and clean. Mind you it was the only thing he did keep clean. If left to his own devises, he wouldn't have had a wash from one month to the next, let alone a bath and as for his bedroom. Well, the less said about that, the better."

"What did Timmy do with the money he had saved, Granddad?" said Stuart.

"I can't really remember what he spent it on." replied his grandfather. "Timmy and money did not stay company for long, his theory was money should be spent. I know he promised his family he would buy them a supper next time

71

the fish and chip van came to the village. This was to thank them for his smashing present. It was going to be fish and chips, but he had spent most of his money, so it was fish cake and chips instead.

"Did they keep their bikes for long time?" asked James.

"Surprisingly, not very long for Timmy; before the new year was halfway through. Circumstances were set to overtake this boy, which was to deny him the use of his bike and many other things. In fact they had only been back to school for a few weeks after the Christmas Holiday, when Tom and Timmy thought they had lost their bikes altogether."

Every night they had been cycling the two and a half miles to a friend's house. Their friend John had received a train set for Christmas. It was not just any old train set, it was not even new, but it was fantastic. There was box, after box, after box, of jumbled up track, rolling stock, stations, buildings, farmyards and all the other paraphernalia that goes to make a great train layout. John's father had made a big L shaped bench in one of the attics, in their large shambling and chaotic old farmhouse.

This house never ceased to amaze Timmy. If you went through a door in the 'living' (for want of another word) room, you were in a cow shed, open another in the cow shed and you were back in another part of the house. Timmy lost his way several times because it took him a long time to work out the shape of the house. Looked at from most angles on the outside, it was just a huge jumble of buildings. These assorted constructions of wood, concrete blocks, bricks, stone, old doors and almost anything else which came to hand; were mostly roofed in rusty corrugated iron. They were scattered around higgledy-pickledy, mostly attached to the main building on the sides and rear; almost completely obscuring what must have been a fine and imposing house. When built the house would have had a sort of horseshoe shape, with two large wings on each side; but its original outlines had long since disappeared. All symmetry affects there might have been in the past had gone and the area between the two wings at the rear was covered and was now part of the working farm. This made some of the rooms at the rear of the house very dark indeed, but the advantage was a covered short cut, from one wing to the other, via the farm buildings in the middle. It was no wonder Timmy was confused and got lost several times.

The occupants of the house were another source of wonder to both Tom and Timmy. John their school mate had lots and lots of brothers and sisters. There seemed to be a whole range from babies to adults, two of whom worked full time on the farm. But there were other people living in the house, who seemed to come and go. What relation, if any, they were to John was never really established, because Tom and Timmy didn't think even John knew. When questioned, he would say, "She's an aunt, or he's a cousin," but it was all rather vague. The thing that struck both Tom and Timmy was the easy-going and friendly feeling, when entering the house. This large chaotic household even seemed to work to a certain extent. Where they did seem to fall down, was collecting the children from the village school. They got them to school OK, but collecting was another thing. One person would think the other was picking them up and in the end no one did. If the transport, which could be anything, from a battered old car, to a tractor and trailer, or even a horse and cart, was not waiting when the children came out of school, weather permitting they started walking. They knew from experience, it might not turn up at all. If it was pouring down with rain they would wait at the school, knowing they would be missed eventually, though some times they had to wait a long time. To counteract this, John would cycle and if the weather was not too bad, when he came out of school, would ride home to raise the alarm. Some sort of transport would be rustled up to go and collect the rest of the children. It was all good-natured and there did not seem to be any recriminations, when the organization went awry.

When Tom and Timmy were visiting, they left their bikes under a wooden veranda that ran along the front of the house. They thought this veranda and the ramshackle buildings along side, made the house look rather like a cowboy saloon in a western town. They pretended they were arriving on horses and it would only have needed the front door to have bat wings for their fantasies to be almost complete. On one memorable occasion there was even a horse tied to the railings, though it was only an old cart horse. One night after they had finished railway building, Tom and Timmy sat for a long time under the veranda, waiting for the rain to ease. It was raining the preverbal cats and dogs and though they had water proofs, it was defiantly not a night for cycling. One of John's elder brothers offered to run them home by car and went in to the house to get the keys.

"I can only find the keys for Jessie," he said when he came out, wearing a Sou'wester and an old mac. "All the other vehicles must be out; so you will have to leave your bikes here, there's not room on Jessie for them." Tom and Timmy looked at each other. Who or what was Jessie? They were soon to find out, Jessie turned out to be a tiny little car, with only two seats. Timmy did not know what make it was, but it was even smaller than an Austin Seven and had a canvass roof that leaked like a sieve; so it was a good job they had their bicycle waterproofs otherwise they would have been drowned.

The next day, Mr Gold the shopkeeper spotted the bikes, while delivering newspapers to the farm. They could not really be missed, because they certainly stood out being the only things visible on these premises that were bright and shiny. While passing the time of the day, with a member of the household, he was informed the bikes had been left the night before and the boys taken home by car, because of the torrential rain. As stated before, Mr Gold was not noted as a kindly man, but he decided to do his good turn for the day and take the bikes back to the village. He had not yet visited Tom and Timmy's homes, so when he did, he could drop the bikes off with the newspapers. School was out and for a change transport was waiting for John and his tribe. Today it was a horse and quite a large cart, which was about a quarter full of hay.

"You might as well come home with us now," shouted John, from the cart, as he spotted Tom and Timmy coming out of the school gates. "There's plenty of room, you can pick up your bikes and come back to my house later, or stay for tea if you like. Mum won't mind." Tom and Timmy looked at each other.

"It sounds a good idea to me," said Tom.

They had planned to use the bike belonging to Timmy's mother to get to John's place and then on the return trip, ride their own bikes and push the adult bike between them. Timmy had not been looking forward to this excursion; riding a bike and pushing another is quite easy and two on a bike may not sound difficult, but for two small boys the journey of several miles on a big ladies bike is a bit tricky. So Timmy agreed with Tom and the invitation of a lift was gratefully accepted, though as much as they would have liked, they would not be able to stay for tea. Tom and Timmy had an easy-going relationship with their respective parents and within reason had almost complete freedom to come and go, or do as they please; but there was one golden rule, both had to obey, or the retributions were terrible. HOME FROM SCHOOL IMMEDIATLY AND GET YOUR GOOD CLOTHES OFF. So they were in trouble already by going to John's place before going home to change. When the horse and cart was the mode of transport it seemed that half the school got on the cart to be dropped off en-route at their respective homes. Tom and Timmy were quite envious and would have liked to join them, but they lived close to the school and in the other direction. Hector the horse was only used on the school run to give him exercise, because he was almost redundant on the farm, tractors having taken over; but he did not seem to like these duties and clumped along at a very slow pace indeed. No amount of inducement could make him go faster than a lethargic plod. In fact when he stopped for children to get off the cart, he would be reluctant to start up again, more interested in eating the grass on the sides of the road. Timmy sat in the cart daydreaming, with his head and arms hanging over the side. It was one of those rare winter evenings with the sun casting long shadows, he thought it was sheer bliss and was almost oblivious to the chatting, joking and singing going on all around him; what a lovely way to go to and from school. He had at the beginning of the journey sat with the driver, but there was only room for one on the seat so had sat by the driver's feet instead. From this position he could not see much, only the rear of Hector, whom he thought was old, big and fat. Hector was indeed an old big fat horse, he was also an old big fat horse with flatulence and where Timmy was sitting was not a good idea at all: he soon went back and sat in the hay with the other children.

Timmy's daydreaming evaporated as they arrived at the farm, when he noticed the look of concern on Tom's face.

"Where's our bikes John?" Tom said with a slight shake in his voice.

"I don't know?" Said John. "They were there this morning when we left for school, I expect someone has put them inside for safekeeping. Tom and Timmy had a look in the sheds and barns, while John went inside to enquire, but the bikes could not be found and nobody had moved them.

"I wonder if they've been pinched by them gypsies that are camped down by the river?" Said Jane, an elder sister of John's.

"Well, if it was them, its too late now, cause I saw 'em leaving," said one of the older brothers. "Twas about eleven o'clock, they were on the road going towards Barton. You'll have to go home and get the serial numbers and tell the police. I don't hold out much hope though, cause they could be anywhere; could have sold'em by now." Tom and Timmy were devastated as once again they were taken home in Jessie. Timmy's top lip was quivering, he was so choked up he could hardly talk. Tom was even worse, he was moaning as if in pain.

Ashen faced and with shaking hands Timmy had trouble opening the garden gate. He could not hold his emotions back any longer, the tears just erupted from his eyes and flooded down his face

"Oh Mum!" He cried as he burst into the kitchen. "We've lost our bikes, the gypsies have pinched them." She looked at him a little bewildered.

"You haven't lost your bike Timmy, go and have a

look in the out-house." The hinges nearly came off the door as Timmy tore it open and there was his bike, as shiny and beautiful as ever.

"How did it get here?" He shouted, tears still streaming down his face.

"Mr Gold saw your bikes while delivering papers and kindly brought them back to save you a journey," she said with a big smile on her face.

"Oh Mum, Oh Mum!" He shouted as he grabbed his mother and danced her around the floor so erratically they almost fell over.

"Oh Mum, I really thought I had lost my bike," he cried, tears still gushing down his face, but now they were tears of joy.

"Let that be a lesson to you, young man," said his mother, after he had changed and sat down for tea. "You have a responsibility to look after your own property; otherwise it will get lost or stolen."

"I know, Mum, I have learnt my lesson," said Timmy, eyes red and puffy from his tears. There is one thing, he thought as he ate his tea; Mum forgot I didn't come home to change my good clothes after school.

The Shrinking Sledge

"What else did the boys get up to now they had bicycles then, Granddad?" said James. "Although you might not have said they terrorised the whole county, you did say no where in the county was safe from their exploits. So what else did they get up to?"

"I should imagine," butted in Stuart. "now they had bikes and could go further afield; the results of their escapades might escape the notice of their parents, the school and people who knew them in the village."

"You're quite right, Stuart," said the grandfather. "It would be the summer before they made really long trips. First of all they had to get over the snow; bikes are not much good in the snow.

"Was there a lot of snow in those days then, Granddad?" said James. "More than we get now?"

"I don't think so," replied the old man, "but now and again there were exceptional years for snow, just as there are now. The year Tom and Timmy finally got their bikes was a good one for snow, or bad whichever way you want to look at it. The snow storms were quite heavy and the wind caused drifting, though the snow did not stay on the ground for too long. One thing was certain though, when the snow eventually came the boys were ready and they loved it."

Would the snow ever come? It had been threatening for days and everyone said it would snow, but it seemed reluctant to come down. Tom and Timmy, with the help of their parents and other elders had made sledges in preparation and were now forlornly looking at the sky.

"What's the use of a sledge if there's no snow?" said Tom as he kicked the object of his derision moodily. "It's just a lump of wood and it hasn't got any use at all; if it doesn't snow soon I'm going to burn it. At least the fire will keep us warm for a while." They had gone to the sloping field to see if the sledges would slide on the wet grass; but of course they wouldn't. David, who had been sitting on the gate watching the two in amusement said, "You couldn't burn my sledge because most of it is made of metal." Tom and Timmy looked at David but did not say anything; they were fed up of hearing about the sledge an uncle had given him.

"If we could find some wheels," replied Timmy thoughtfully, trying to ignore David as he sat shivering on his sledge, "we might be able to turn the sledges into carts."

"That's an idea," said Tom and so, muffled up to the eyebrows against the cold they set off on their bikes to badger friends and neighbours for old pram wheels.

Several hours of cajoling and begging only resulted in three wheels, which was no good at all.

"What's the use of three wheels?" said Tom as he and Timmy sat in John's kitchen drinking a hot mug of milk. John's farm had been their last and best hope of finding wheels, but after much searching by John and others in his family only three wheels could be found.

"Oh well, if we can't build carts," said Timmy. "Why don't we carry on building John's model railway?" Reluctantly Tom agreed and they all trooped up into the attic and were soon absorbed in constructing bridges, stations, level crossings and other paraphernalia for a model railway. So much so that when John's mother called them for tea, they were surprised to see it was dark and even more surprised to be told it was snowing. Not just any old snow, it was huge flakes that were falling, you could not see across the farmyard, it was almost like a blizzard. All thoughts of tea were gone as they hurriedly put on their boots, they almost threw on their outdoor clothes which included, gloves, scarves and bobble hats. Outside the whole farm was being transformed, from a sea of mud, ramshackle old buildings and rusting machinery into a scene of pure white beauty. Not that Tom and Timmy noticed this very much as they were soon engaged in a serious snowball fight with John, his brothers and sisters; even his mum and dad joined in. When they were all whacked out John's mother suggested her husband took Tom and Timmy home on the tractor and trailer, but the boys would have none of that; they wanted to ride home in the snow. So they set off, with almost the whole of the farmer's family standing in the snow waving and shouting their goodbye's, a few snowballs were lobbed to help them on their way. Tom and Timmy had only cycled a few yards before the two outside lights of the farm had disappeared altogether, they then realised just how dark it was; their puny front lights hardly penetrated the falling snow. They were slipping and sliding all over the place and although they knew the road well, were soon quite disorientated. Once or twice they almost went into a ditch and so decided to walk; even so they almost had a couple of calamities with missed corners and walking the wrong side of a small bridge. But they loved it, imagining they were on an expedition to the North Pole, or heading for the base camp to climb Mount Everest. They arrived outside Timmy's house OK and were making arrangements for the following day when they were surprised to see Tom's mother coming out of the door. She had been to see if Tom was at his friend's house. It was only one of the few times that Timmy could remember their parents showing any signs of them being worried about being late home; they were normally just told off, or got some other form of punishment. When Timmy's mother explained why she and Tom's mother were so anxious he could see the reason for their consternation. It was now snowing more than ever and with the increasing wind it really was blizzard conditions.

"You and Tom go a long way on your bikes, don't you?" she said.

"Yes," said Timmy, "but that doesn't normally worry you Mum."

"I know Timmy," she replied, "but look at the weather; you could be anywhere in the county, or further for all we know; if you hadn't come home and we had to start searching for you, where on earth would we start?"

"But we were only at Johns house, Mum," said Timmy.

"I know that now, Timmy," she said with rising anger. "You two must show more consideration. How were we to know you were at John's house? We don't get a lot of snow in this part of the country but in conditions like this you must stay locally and by locally I mean in the village. I want to know where you are going and what time you will be back; and another thing, I want you home on time for your meals in future. Is that clear young man." Her flushed face was only inches from Timmy's and she was almost shouting.

"Yes Mum," said Timmy, suitably chastised; she didn't get mad at him very often, but when she did watch out. He kept a very low profile for the rest of the evening; staying in his room for most of the time.

Sunday morning and both Tom and Timmy were up at

the crack of dawn. Timmy could hardly wait for his
breakfast, so impatient was he to get out. He gobbled
down his food, which earned a rebuke from his mother;
but nothing could quell his excitement as he threw on his
coat and ran outside. The blizzard of the evening before
had subsided and now only a few whispy flakes were
falling, but it looked overcast as if there was a lot more
snow to come down. Not that it was needed, thought
Timmy because boy! was the snow deep. The wind had
blown the snow into drifts against the hedges and walls

and in some places it was
plastered against houses,
trees and telegraph poles.
Timmy had never seen
snow like this before; the
shear beauty and
grandeur of the sights
which he came across as
he made his way along
the road towards Tom's
house took his breath
away. It was still early
and because it was Sunday the snow was still pristine, not
another soul had walked along the road before Timmy.
What a pity I've spoilt that new snow, thought Timmy
when he had reached Tom's gate and turned to look at his
footprints all along the middle of the road. Tom did not
have any of Timmy's inhibitions about spoiling the snow
when he came out; he jumped into the first drift, threw
snowballs and generally ran around like a lunatic until he
was out of breath. The two boys then went to look for the
sledges which they had discarded as useless only the day
before.

"What a good job we didn't burn them or turn them

83

into carts," said Timmy as they headed for the field where they had left them the day before.

"That reminds me," replied Tom. "Someone left an old pram at our house while we were out yesterday. So when the snow has gone we can turn at least one of them into a cart."

The look on their faces would have been worth recording as they climbed over the gate and into the field where the sledges had been discarded. They had left what Tom had called those useless lumps of wood, somewhere near the bottom of the field. The bottom of this field was now covered in a huge snowdrift.

"Where do you think we left them?" said Timmy with the dismayed look still on his face.

"I think they were over there," replied Tom heading in the direction he had indicated; the snow already waist-deep and getting deeper. Floundering about in the drift, with snow sometimes deeper than the boys, they were getting nowhere. After about twenty minuets of futile searching they went back and sat on the gate to catch their breath.

"What we need are shovels," declared Tom, "let's go home and get some." So they went back home to get shovels. Tom's mother thought he wanted a shovel to clear the path.

"I'll do that when we have found our sledges," he shouted as he jumped the small drift which had formed near the garden gate. I'll believe that when it happens, she thought as she watched him walk away with Timmy by his side. With the shovels on their shoulders, she thought they looked like two diminutive workmen as they disappeared around the corner of the road. Although snow is light the shovels were big and these were only two small boys who were very soon getting out of puff, as they flailed away in the snowdrift. It wasn't long before Tom and Timmy were back sitting on the gate; whacked out and feeling very dejected as they contemplated the next move. It was then that David came along pulling his brand new sledge; he was heading for the hill.

"Just the man!" shouted Timmy as he grabbed David by the arm and started to drag him towards the gate. "Can you remember where we left our sledges?"

"Well, yes of course I can," said David as he climbed the gate; he pointed his finger. "You left them over there, where it looks like you have been digging."

"But they're not there!" shouted Tom.

"I know that," said David with a broad grin on his face. "You said where did you leave them, and that's where you left them, but they're not there now." Tom and Timmy looked at him in bewilderment.

"Well where are they?" They shouted almost in unison. David laughed and turned to look at Tom.

"You said you were going to burn them," he said. "When I told my Dad he told me to go and collect them, as they would make good kindling wood."

"Thank goodness for that," said Timmy. "Let's go and fetch them Tom."

"You had better hurry then," said David with obvious mirth, the huge grin on his face was now almost stretching from ear to ear. "When I left home Dad was in the shed and it sounded as if he was chopping up fire wood." Tom and Timmy dropped their shovels and, slipping and sliding in the snow, they made a dash for David's house. David followed the Two T's at a more leisurely pace; he just wanted to see what would happen next, he was enjoying this. Tom and Timmy were too bigheaded by half, he thought and he had said so quite often; this to anyone who would listen. Before they even reached David's house they could hear banging coming from the shed, they almost flew down the path and burst into the shed; much to the surprise of David's father. David's father was indeed chopping up wood and there on the floor was a huge pile of kindling wood, the result of an hour or so work.

"Is that our sledges?" blurted out Tom as he and Timmy stared in dismay at the pile of wood. David's father looked rather puzzled.

"I don't know what you mean?" he said. "It's just a pile of kindling wood.

"Yes, but was it our sledges before you chopped them up?" cried Timmy.

"No, of course I didn't chop up your sledges," he said. "It was I who gave your parents the wood to make them in the first place; so why would I chop them up? When it started snowing last night," he continued "I told David to go and fetch them, because if it snowed all night, which it did, you might have trouble finding them in the morning. The sledges are around the side of the shed, leaning against the wall." Tom and Timmy looked at each other incredulously. They then heard laughter from outside and went out to be met by the site of David, hanging on to the gate for support; he was almost bent double in his mirth, there was actually tears running down his face. Oh boy, how he was enjoying this.

"You should have seen your faces." He gasped before giving way to another bout of laughter. "How I'll love telling this to the gang. Oh and there's school tomorrow." He wheezed before breaking down again.

"You just wait, David!" said Tom as he dragged his sledge up the path. We'll get you for this." And it wasn't long before the opportunity came about, though not in the way Tom and Timmy had envisaged or wanted.

Tom and Timmy started to drag their sledges up

towards the hill, which was about three quarters of a mile away. In many ways the children of this village, which was situated on the edge of the levels, were lucky when it snowed. At least they had a hill which was quite good for tobogganing; whereas most of the villages out on the levels or moors were on dead flat land. Though some were situated on small rises or hillocks which were once islands before the moors were drained, and so had small toboggan runs. Even before the boys reached the top of the hill, they could hear shouting, laughter and screaming coming from the other side. This makeshift sledge run was situated on the far side of the hill from the village, so they could not see who it was making all the noise. Timmy was in the front as he and Tom came over the brow and the sight before him made him stop in his tracks; resulting in Tom stumbling into Timmy's sledge.

"What did you stop for?" demanded Tom.

"Just look at this," said Timmy as Tom joined him at the top of the hill. There before them was an incredulous scene. It seemed to Timmy that every child from miles around was gathered here on the far side of the hill. There were of course one or two mums and dads with small children. There were also one or two grown ups without children who were just there to have a go on a sledge. (Some people never seem to grow up, thank goodness)

"I reckon there are more children here than go to our school," said Tom in awe. The boys rushed down to join in and had great fun. Sometimes lying down, sometimes going backwards and sometimes even trying to stand up as they hurtled down the hill. Most people had homemade sledges, but some had large metal trays and even a piece of corrugated iron was in use. This lump of metal was big enough to hold several riders at a time and would spin round and round, sometimes tipping up. Not many people would be left sitting or lying on it when it reached the bottom. It was great exhilarating fun going down.

"But its blooming hard work pulling the sledge back up," puffed Tom, trying to get his breath back, as he lay panting in the snow on the top of the hill. It was now well past midday and people were starting to leave for Sunday dinner. Tom and Timmy would have loved to stay longer, but hunger beckoned so reluctantly they decided to go home.

"We should have brought sandwiches with us." Said Timmy.

"That would have been a good idea," replied Tom as they started off for home. "But we will be back this afternoon, won't we?"

"Yes," said Timmy, he then stopped and looked at Tom. "So why are we taking our sledges home when we'll only have to drag them back up again?"

"You're dead right, Timmy," said Tom. "Let's take them back and leave them on the top." So this is what they did; leaving the sledges stacked one on top of the other in a corner of the field. It was then they realised that a lot of other people had done the same. There were abandoned sledges all over the place, with only a few people now tobogganing. Among the abandoned sledges was David's. Oh how he had shown off when parading this vehicle; particularly to Tom and Timmy who had tried hard but not very successfully to show any envy, but in reality they were almost green. The runners and framework on this magnificent sledge were made of tubular metal and painted bright blue and the wooden slats a garish pink alternating with a brilliant yellow. The whole gaudy edifice was topped with two six foot aerials at the back with fluttering red pennants on the top.

"It looks like an American Cadillac in a car park of

Austin Sevens," was the comment the boys had overheard as they had pulled their sledges up the hill. This shop bought sledge looked very light and it certainly went faster and further than any of the homemade ones. Tom and Timmy looked at each other; they both knew what the other was thinking.

"You go first then Tom," said Timmy. So Tom had the first ride, then Timmy had his go and then they went down together; it certainly was a good sledge. The few other children still on the hill were now taking an interest and on the next trip down there were five bodies on the

sledge, piled one on top of the other. This was not a good idea because halfway down it tipped up; spilling the occupants all over the place. Nobody was hurt but when they righted the

sledge they saw with horror that both aerials were crumpled.

"It's your fault," said one of the girls who had been an occupant of the sledge; she was pointing her finger at Tom and Timmy. "You two started it, so you can take the blame." With that she grabbed the hand of her younger brother and marched off. The others on the hill were strangely disappearing quite quickly as well. Soon the only people on the hill were Tom and Timmy who, with mixed results, were trying to straighten the aerials. They had managed to mend one so there was hardly a kink in it but the other had almost broken in half when they had tried to straighten in out. To top it all it was now snowing again and their hands were freezing.

"Well we can't fix it," said Tom. "Anyway I'm hungry, so let's go home for dinner." All the way through dinner, which Timmy was eating on his own; the others in the family having finished a long time ago, he tried to think of a remedy for the damaged sledge. He had a furtive imagination but nothing would come to mind. In the end it was the weather which came to their rescue; the snow that had been threatening all morning was now beginning fall and the wind was getting up.

"You're not going out in that young man." His mother had said, as she saw Timmy putting in his coat.

"But Mum, our sledges are still on he top of the hill," cried Timmy.

"You can get them when it has stopped," she replied. "And even if it doesn't stop this afternoon they will still be there tomorrow." Timmy began to realise their good fortune. If the weather was too bad for them to fetch their sledges then David would probably have to leave his sledge on the hill as well. Later that afternoon there was a knock on the door and there in the porch was John.

"Mum said, do you and Tom want to come to our house for tea?" He said shaking the snow off his hat. Timmy looked in awe at the weather outside; John must have seen the look of consternation on his face because he said, "its OK we don't have to walk; Dad and Tim are up on the road with the tractor and trailer. We've been to feed the cattle and he said he will bring you back." With pleading eyes Timmy turned to look at his mother who had joined him on the door step.

"Yes you can go, Timmy," she said. "I don't mind if you're with an adult and you have got transport." Once again Timmy threw on his boots and outdoor clothes, then ran along the road to Tom's house. Tom's mother could hardly refuse Tom permission to go to John's house as Timmy was going; so it wasn't long before the three of them were climbing up on the trailer. Tim sat with his father on the tractor and the boys sat at the back of the trailer with their legs dangling over the edge. Singing at the top their voices, they made a very happy tableau and brought many faces to windows as their transport bumped along the country lanes. It was not snowing very hard but every now and again when the wind dropped there was a really heavy flurry. It was in one of these that they noticed vehicle lights coming out of the snow and then disappear. The lights then appeared again and the trio started waving and shouting; they didn't want the car or whatever it was to bump into them. When the vehicle had drawn close enough for them to just make out the shape of a car; it inexplicitly swerved into a ditch. John got up and ran to the front of the trailer to inform his father and Tim of the drama that had happened behind. Tim jumped off the tractor before it had stopped and ran back; the boys and John's father following as quickly as they could. When the boys and John's father arrived on the scene they could see the car had not gone right into the ditch, but was languishing on the grass verge at quite a precarious angle; with only one wheel in the ditch. A man and a woman who must have been the occupants of the car were now standing in the middle of the road with Tim. Although they appeared to be unharmed they seemed rather animated; Tim was saying, "Well, we were only just in front of you and we didn't see anything?"

John's father assessed the situation, and said with a big grin on his face. "There will be no problem at all in getting this car out of the ditch." They could all hear him chuckling as he went to get the tractor and trailer. With the help of a rope which always seemed to be on the trailer; true to his word, the car was back on the road in no time at all. While Tim was undoing the rope attached to the car he said to the couple, "We're going to pull in at a gateway along the road so you can pass us."

The boys jumped back up on the trailer ready to depart and as they did so, Timmy noticed strange looks being passed between the man and the woman. The car passed the tractor and trailer as planned and they thought very little more of the incident.

The story the couple told in the public house that evening caused great hilarity.

"We were making our way very gingerly along the lane, because the snow was suddenly quite heavy," said the man, "when something seemed to be taking shape in front of us. I slowed down and it disappeared; so I speeded up again and three grotesque little figures appeared floating in the air about four feet from the ground. They were waving their arms about, shouting and gesticulating in a frenzied manner; Jane screamed and I swerved; ending up with the front wheel stuck in the ditch. We thought we were just lucky when Jack and Tim Higgs turned up out of the snow and offered to pull us out. It was only when those three kids jumped up on the trailer when we were leaving that we both realised what we had seen. It was getting dark and the trailer did not have any lights; also the back of that trailer sticks out a long way from the wheels. The lights on my car are not all that good and they were probably covered in snow as well making things worse. This and the sudden flurry of snow meant that we could only see those three little monkeys, seemingly hovering in the air; the trailer they we sitting on was almost invisible. We did feel stupid but I tell you we were both still shaking when we got home and I don't think it was from almost going in the ditch either."

The boys had a great afternoon putting the model railway together but that was almost an anticlimax to the smashing tea. The tea, like everything else in this family was informal and was set out on a huge table with any number of people sat around it. It was at this table that Tom and Timmy told of their woes with David's sledge. Their story was greeted with a lot of laughter and unhelpful suggestions, but there was not any malice in the jollity and Tom and Timmy joined in and gave as good as they got. In the end Jack, another older brother of John's said he might be able to help; he was, he said, going near the hill in the morning to feed cattle and he would have a look at the sledge when he had finished. Tom and Timmy were now quite hopeful because John's father and elder brothers always seemed to be fixing something on the farm; they seemed to be able to mend anything.

It was afternoon and school had finished at last. Tom and Timmy were the first out of the building.

"See you in a minute," shouted Tom as he ran past Timmy's house. They wanted to be the first on the hill; they certainly wanted to be there before David. Tom was in the lead as they made their way up the hill and there was a cry of joy as he disappeared over the brow.

"He's fixed it!" He shouted, "he's fixed it!" He shouted again. Sure enough he had fixed it. But Timmy thought there was something wrong as he walked around the sledge several times; and then it dawned on him what it was.

"The aerials are shorter," he said incredulously. "They're not even the same length."

"So they are," said Tom.

John's brother was later to describe just how he had fixed the aerials.

"I just undid the brackets which held the aerials in place, cut off the damaged bits with a hacksaw and stuck them back in; it only took me a few minutes."

"Do you think David will notice?" said Tom.

"He probably will," said Timmy. "What he will notice is that his sledge is the only one not covered in snow and there are footprints all around it."

"Well, let's clear the snow off all the sledges, we can say we were just getting them ready for use," said Tom.

"What a good idea," replied Timmy as he hurriedly cleared the snow off the first sledge. They were none too soon because David was the first to arrive and he was rather surprised to see Tom and Timmy getting sledges ready for others to use.

"What are you two doing?" he said suspiciously.

"Just preparing the sledges for the others," said Timmy.

"Well I don't want you to prepare my sledge; in fact I don't want either of you two touching my sledge." With that he gave his sledge a push, jumped on and went sailing down the hill.

"He didn't notice!" gasped a relieved Tom. And indeed he hadn't but later on they saw him looking at his sledge in a rather bemused fashion and scratching his head.

"My aerials have shrunk," he said when he had reached the top after about his third trip.

"Different to his head, then," said Tom looking at Timmy with a big grin on his face. He was having a job to stop laughing. Timmy however did not have Tom's will power.

"You shouldn't have left it out all night," he spluttered, he was now almost helpless with laughter. "You know what shop bought things are like, it probably does not like the cold."

"Don't be so stupid!" snapped David. "I think you two have got something to do with this."

"How could we?" said Tom. "We left school the same time as you; we had only been here a few minutes before you arrived."

How could they indeed? It remained a mystery for ever more.

The Old Man of the Moors

Far out on the moors lived an old man in an isolated house. He was probably not all that old, but he seemed old to Tom and Timmy who thought most grown ups were old and some, like this man who lived alone on the moors, were very old indeed. He was the moorkeeper and was employed by the farmers in the area. One of his many jobs was to check the cattle twice a day; making sure none had fallen into the big rhynes that drained the moors. Any animal falling into one of these large ditches or rhynes as  the drainage channels are called on the Somerset Levels; would have difficulties getting out unaided and would sometimes be horned by the other beasts. Come rain or sunshine, winter or summer, he seemed to be attired in the same clothes. With his greasy old cap, a raincoat that was ripped all down one side and held together with string, he would traverse the moors, on a rickety battered old bike. The old man went about his business with an unlit pipe permanently stuck in his mouth and a large stick across the handlebars of his bike. This large stick and his inability to ride in a straight line made it difficult for other users of the road to pass him. Peddling with only one leg, the other being stiff and sometimes sticking out at an alarming angle; he made a familiar site to the villagers as they crossed the moors, when going to the local town.

Tom and Timmy often wondered if this leg was wooden or just stiff from some accident or other that had happened sometime in the past. Whatever the reason for his stiff leg, he would not communicate it to Tom and Timmy. He was not a very communative man at the best of times and would have no words at all to say to the village children. Boys in particular he regarded as less than vermin and Tom and Timmy were the worst of the lot. Now they had bicycles, the far moors and the old man's area were within easy reach. Boys can be very cruel and one of Tom and Timmy's favourite pastimes was to try and mimic the old man, as he went about his business. They would ride behind him on their bicycles, one-legged, the same as he did; the hardest bit was trying to anticipate the next swerve. This would sometimes go on for a mile or two, or until the old man got fed up and would take a swipe at them with his big stick. He once actually caught Tom with the stick and it was quite a hefty thwack; this seemed to curb the activity of mimicry quite a lot.

One day, coming back from an expedition to the local town, Tom and Timmy passed the old man on his bicycle going the other way with his dog. This was unusual, because the animal normally stayed at home, acting as a guard dog.

"He must be going to tend sheep," said Timmy. They had noticed he only had the dog with him when he had to look after sheep; which was not very often as sheep were rarely put on the moors. The land was prone to flooding resulting in wet and marshy conditions, this made it unsuitable for sheep who are susceptible to foot rot.

97

"Now's our opportunity to take a look at his house," said Tom. They had often wondered about his bleak, scruffy-looking house in the middle of the moors; as did a lot of people. It was situated next to a large rhyne, miles from the nearest house and was without electricity or water. The boys hid their bikes before they got to the house, because they did not want anyone to see them outside of the building. Keeping an eye out and their ears open in case the old man came back, they sneaked through the broken-down gate and tried to look through the nearest window. It was so dark inside and the window was so dirty they could not see a thing. They tried the next window with the same result. The front door was their next target and this opened with a slight creaking sound.

"This must be his bedroom," whispered Tom. There was an unmade bed against one wall. A chest of drawers and a few chairs made up the rest of the furniture; there were piles of clothes on the floor, on the drawers and on the chairs. Almost directly opposite was an opening with a dim light filtering through, they made their way towards it, picking their way between the piles of clothes. The opening was a doorway without a door and led into what they assumed was the kitchen. In the corner was what looked like a paraffin cooker, but it was to dark to be sure. In front of a grimy window with the remnants of curtains hanging down on one side, was a stone washbasin with draining boards on both sides. The two draining boards were piled high with clutter and perched one of these piles of clutter was a pure white cat, looking disdainfully down at the boys. Timmy began to feel a little troubled. Although the pair of them had seemed to do a lot of trespassing just lately and it had not worried him; this was something different, it was private and he was feeling uncomfortable.

"We shouldn't be in here," he whispered. "Let's go."

"I want to see more," said Tom.

"Well I don't," said Timmy as he made his way to the door. Reluctantly Tom followed.

"What's the matter with you?" he wanted to know of his friend, when they were back outside.

"I don't really know?" said Timmy. "It's hard to explain; the place was in such a mess, I don't know how anyone can live in a mess like that. Yet it's his mess, his house, and I somehow felt ashamed to be in there looking at it." Tom looked at Timmy and shook his head. Timmy was up for almost any caper and a lot of the scrapes and troubles they had been in recently had been instigated by Timmy, with his unbelievable imagination and curiosity. Yet sometimes his friend's deep thoughts and sensitivities caught him by surprise, they were quite beyond his comprehension.

"Well, can we go and see what he's got in those sheds, then?" Tom asked scornfully still shaking his head.

"OK," said Timmy, pretending not to notice Tom's disdainful tone, or the shaking of his head and the aggrieved look on his face. The first shed only had chopped logs in it, so they went round the other side of the house where there was a large lean-to, the whole length of the main building. The big double doors were held closed by a large piece of wood; this piece of wood was held at one end by a single nut and bolt, the other resting in a hasp on the opposite door. They lifted this large wooden latch and stepped inside expecting to find heaps of junk as in the main house. When their eyes had grown familiar to the gloom, they were surprised to find it housed loads and loads of tools and implements, mostly for farming and stock management, also for hedging and ditching. There were rolls of wire, stakes and other paraphernalia for electric fencing. Many of the tools they could only guess at their use, others they didn't have a clue what they were for, or how they were supposed to be used. While the lads were trying to work out the use of a three-wheeled implement which had a seat on one side; the door closed with a bang and they heard the piece of wood being dropped into place. The large shed was now in almost complete blackness, the only light filtering through a tiny spider web covered window at the far end and around the loose fitting doors. Tom and Timmy shouted and ran towards the door, tripping over tools and other obstacles in their path. They pushed against the doors, although the doors gave a bit to their shoving and heaving, the big piece of wood held firm.

"Come on, let us out!" shouted Tom. But there was no reply.

"Please let us out," pleaded Timmy.

"Yes please open the door and let us out," chimed in Tom. "We're sorry to be trespassing and we won't do it again so please let us out." They pleaded to be let out and then threatened him with their dads, but it was all to no avail, there was complete silence from the other side of the door; the old man had not uttered one word.

"It's as if he just closed the door and then gone away," said Timmy. And that in fact is just what he had done. When the boys had passed him, he had remembered he had not locked the front door. He didn't trust those two boys with very good reason; he had stopped, turned around and followed them. He could not of course catch them; but on these open flat moors you could see for miles and he had seen them hide their bikes and go on foot towards his house, so he knew they were up to no good. Finding them in his shed was too good an opportunity to miss. Creeping up to the doors, he had closed the one that was open and dropped the wood down in the hasp. At last he had captured those two tiresome boys and he wasn't about to free them either. It was a very self-satisfied old man who had got back on his bike and gone about his interrupted business.

"Maybe he's deaf and didn't hear us," added Timmy.

"No he heard us OK," said Tom. "We know he's not deaf; he's probably just getting his own back on us for pestering him. We'll have to break out of here somehow," he added as he looked around. Their eyes were now becoming accustomed to what was at first seemed almost complete darkness; they could just make out the objects in the shed. The only thing that seemed to be missing in this collection of tools was a ladder; so the little window at the far end was probably out as an escape route.

"Well even if there's not a ladder, with all these tools we should be able to get out somehow," said Timmy. "What about that lump of wood which keeps the doors closed? We might be able to undo the nut from this side." When they had been rummaging about, they had found a large wooden box, or chest, which was full of huge rusting spanners. Tom and Timmy sorted through the box and finding a couple of spanners they thought might fit, took them over to the door. The very first one they tried did actually fit; but it was all to no avail, the bolt turned as well as the nut.

"It's no good," said Tom, "even if we could stop the bolt turning, I don't think we would be able to get the nut off, it looks pretty rusty to me." They stood back and looked at the big doors, hoping for an inspiration.

"You can just see the piece of wood that holds the doors shut through the gap," said Timmy.

"So what?" said Tom. "We can't get a hand through to lift it."

"No we can't," replied Timmy. "But we might be able to find something that is thin and strong enough to do it." The boys began to rummage through the piles of equipment and the tools, most of which were hanging on the walls. They found many things they thought would do the trick, but most were either too thick to go through the gap or were too flimsy to lift the big wooden hasp. At last Timmy found something he knew would do the trick; it was a scythe. For a tool that looks so ungainly, ugly and awkward, a scythe is a beautiful implement to use. With it's large slightly curved blade which can be honed to a very fine sharpness, the subtle shape of the handle and movable grips which can be adjusted to suit any size or shape of person; makes it, to coin a modern terminology, a really user-friendly instrument. The minimum of energy is required to cut large swathes of grass, thistles or corn in a very short time. The users of spluttering or whining strimmers do not know what they are missing. Of course the boys were not going to use the scythe for mowing, its large blade which was quite thin at the end, made it ideal to poke through the gap of the doors and lift the piece of wood out of the hasp. The blade of the scythe went through the gap OK, but the wood seemed to be stuck in the hasp, try as they might it would not move. Tom kicked the door in frustration.

"Why won't the darn thing move?" He said giving the door another good kicking in his annoyance. It then dawned on him why it wouldn't move.

"When we were first trying to get out, we were pushing the doors outwards and that's what has pinched the wood in the hasp," he explained to Timmy. "If we pull the doors back it should make the wood free in the hasp." So this is what they did, whether it made the wood free or not they couldn't tell because pulling the door back pinched the blade of the scythe in-between the two doors and they couldn't move it. There were tears of frustration in Tom's eyes, as he gave the doors another good kicking.

"Tom, Tom stop. I know how we can do it!" shouted Timmy. "We can use some of that wire, it should be easy." It was now Timmy's turn to do the explaining and Tom, ever the optimist agreed it should be easy. The rolls of wire in question were hanging on big hooks at the far end of the shed and picking their way through all the tools and implements in the near dark was no easy task. The first they tried to lift down was far too heavy for two small boys to manage. This set Tom's frustration off again, but luckily Timmy found a roll of only a few strands; so the door was safe from another kicking. They pushed the doors which released the scythe blade and exposed the offending piece of wood. The wire was poked through the gap in the doors over the top of the wood. Because it had been coiled up for years and retained its hoop-like shape, it came back through the gap under the wood, just as Timmy had said it would. That was the easy bit; the hard bit was trying to tie a knot in it, which was no easy task for small hands. They succeeded though and with the aid of a large wooden rake managed to get the remainder of the wire over the top of one of the doors. Tom pulled the doors together and Timmy pulled on the wire which was free; there being quite a large gap at the top of the door. It worked beautifully, the wood lifted out of the hasp and a gentle push sent the doors wide open, letting in the wonderful fresh air. Running outside and blinking in the bright sunshine, they jumped around laughing and hugging each other. Arm-in-arm and congratulating each other on outsmarting the old man, Tom and Timmy set off to retrieve their bicycles.

But the bicycles were not where they had hidden them.

"That blooming old man must have moved them," wailed Tom.

"Well they can't be far," said Timmy. "Wherever he's put them it's got to be in walking distance hasn't it?"

"Yeah, I suppose you're right." Moaned Tom. So they set about looking for their bikes. After half an hour's searching to no avail they were getting desperate and were back on the road looking under the bridge when a coal lorry came along and stopped.

"What are you two boys up to?" said the driver, who himself was not much more than a boy. Though a big strong boy he was with all his shovelling of coal and humping of full bags; Trev threw them about as if they were feather pillows. He liked Tom and Timmy, laughing at stories of their antics, which were quite often enhanced with the telling. He had even helped them with one of their latest escapades. The boys had played football against the next village and had won five nil. Tom and Timmy had had made a banner proclaiming their famous victory but were having trouble putting it up over the road. They had one side tied to a tree but the tree on the other side did not have any lower branches and the ladder they had borrowed

 was not high enough. It was then Trev had come along and given them a hand. The ladder was plenty long enough when placed on the lorry and the banner was soon in place, billowing in the wind. It was not until Trev and his lorry had gone that they realised the banner was upside down and they did not have any way of rectifying it. Not only was it upside down but it

was starting to rain and the words which had been made with boot polish began to run; so that it looked like a foreign language. With the exception of Trev, nobody in the village knew what it meant or who had put it up there. In the end a man from the council took it down.

"Well, it can't be our boys, this time," said Tom's mother as she leaned over the garden gate talking to Timmy's parents. "It's much too high for them to be involved."

"Mm," said Timmy's father, although Timmy had vehemently denied any involvement, he wasn't so sure.

Tom and Timmy told Trev about their predicament and he helped them look for their bikes; but he was no more successful than they had been. It was now getting rather gloomy and after another half an hour of fruitless searching they decided to call it a day.

"I'll give you a lift home," said Trev. "Tomorrow you can have another look after you have finished school. If you talk to the old man nicely he might tell you where he has hidden them." Tom and Timmy accepted the lift, but were sceptical about the old man giving them their bikes back. They could not enlist the help of their parents either because they had been seen pestering the old man and both sets of parents had warned the boys to keep away from him and leave him alone. So the loss of the bikes had to be kept a secret or they would be in serious trouble. But trouble never seemed to be far away and it happened next day while they were at school.

Their mate Trev had to go to town again the next day to pick up more coal from the station. On the way he drove very slowly in the proximity of the old man's house, trying unsuccessfully to locate the lost bikes.

"I'll stop on the way back," he said to himself and this is what he did; stopping on the bridge outside of the old man's house. He climbed up onto the top of the lorry cab to get a better view of the area and from this vantage point had instant success. There, just below the surface of the big rhyne which ran past the house, were the two bikes.

"Well the nasty old man," said Trev, who was well known for talking to himself. "If I hadn't stood on top of my lorry I don't think they would ever have been found." He was really pleased with himself as he looked for something to fish the bikes out of the water. "This will make the boys happy," he almost shouted with pleasure as he threw the bikes up on the back of the lorry. So once again the bicycles were returned home while Tom and Timmy were at school, but this time they were not the gleaming machines the boys were so proud of. Oh no, they were streaming wet, muddy and festooned with water weed. Trev dumped the bikes in Timmy's garden and shouted through the open back door.

"Timmy and Tom's bikes are in the garden Mrs Richards; tell the boys the old man chucked them in the rhyne."

"What on earth are you talking about, Trev?" She said as she came out of the house wiping her hands on a tea towel.

"It's the boys' bikes Mrs," he said as climbed up into his cab. "The old man on the moors chucked them in that big rhyne next to his house. Didn't the boys tell you?"

"No, they didn't," she said as she marched up the path and through the open gate, heading for Tom's house. "Thanks very much though, Trev, it was very nice of you to return them. Those two boys don't deserve a friend like you."

As the boys neared Timmy's house after school, they sensed something was wrong. It was not that Tom's mother was talking to Timmy's at the garden gate; there was nothing unusual about that. It was their attitude that gave the boys a sense of foreboding.

"Where is your bike, Timmy?" said Timmy's mother. Timmy turned red and didn't answer.

"And where's your bike, Tom?" said Tom's mother. Tom didn't answer either. What could he say? They looked at each other scraping their feet in the gravel and squirming; wondering what was going to come next.

"Come on, Timmy, where is your bike?" said Timmy's mother.

"I don't know," murmured Timmy.

"Speak up, boy. Did you say, you don't know?"

"Yes Mum, we've lost them," said Timmy feeling wretched.

"Then you had better come around here and look in the garden," she said with a glint of anger in her eye. Heads down, they trooped around the hedge through the gate and into the garden. There leaning against the hedge looking in a very forlorn state, were the two bikes.

"Pick that bike up and get home with it," said Tom's mother. As he bent to pick up the bike he got a whack across the back of the head. He would have got another but he saw it coming and managed to duck. "Wait for me up on the road," she said to Tom as he ran across the lawn with his bike. Timmy watched his friend and mother walk along the road. He could hear her raised voice and every now and again she would give Tom another whack as if to emphasise a point. With trepidation Timmy turned to pick up his own bike, he knew he had the same sort of thing coming.

There was one thing though. They never messed with The Old Man of the Moors again.

"How come Timmy didn't keep his bike for very long, Granddad?" said James. "I would have thought that after all the effort he went to try and buy that bike, he would have kept it for ever."

"Well, that is another story," said the old man. "And it is one I don't have time to tell you tonight. Your parents will be here soon so let's watch the television for a while; because I want to see the news."

Plums

The grandparents were babysitting again, though they would not have said so in front of Stuart and James, because the two boys were definitely not babies. The boys had been given strict instructions by their parents, on the exact time they had to go to bed: but when the time came, every excuse imaginable was made not to do so. In exasperation the grandmother said, "If you go to bed now, I will send your Grandfather up to tell you one of his tales." This bribe seemed to do the trick; because they were soon in bed, but sitting up wanting expectantly.

"Well, that was nice of you to volunteer me for that job," said the grandfather"

"Get on with you," she said. "You know you love telling them your daft stories. Why they listen to you, I just don't know." And so he went up to their bedroom and regaled them with more tales of the Troublesome Twosome, the two lads from bygone days.

The Troublesome Twosome or Two T's lived in a large village; not in population, but in size. In reality, it was a collection of two or three villages or hamlets that straggled out over a large area and was situated on the edge of the Somerset Levels. They lived at the bottom end and did not go to the top of the village very often, being drawn to the river and the open flat moors with its moorhens, ducks, and occasional otter. On this occasion though they were at the top end of the village; meeting with friends who were going to show them where several plum trees were growing. Their guides led them across a large orchard. On the far side was an overgrown hedge with a gap about half way. On reaching the gap, a bridge over quite a big ditch was revealed, well, not a proper bridge, just a plank of wood. About thirty yards on the other side were the plum trees. But, it was not the plum

 trees that took Tom and Timmy's attention; it was a caravan, the strangest caravan they had ever seen. It was just like a shed on wheels. The grey wooden walls went straight up to a curved roof, the big wheels seemed to have thin solid rubber tyres, it was quite high, with five or six steps leading up to the door. They were not even sure if it was a caravan. John and Ray, the guides assured our comrades it was indeed a caravan and in it lived a fierce old man, called Albert Bush, the owner of the plum trees.

"Well how do we get the plums?" whispered Timmy. "We throw apples at the caravan," replied Ray. "If he's in, he'll come out and chase us, and for an old man he's very quick. If he's out we leave a lookout on the bridge in case he comes home." Tom did not think a lot of this idea, because there was something wrong with Timmy, he could not run so fast these days. In fact Timmy was not even allowed to ride his beloved red bike; it had been locked away in the shed, so he could not be tempted.

Then Tom had a brainwave.

"If someone crept up to the caravan," he said, "and

then moved the steps, it'll take Albert Bush a long time to get out, especially if he's as old as you say he is." They all thought this was a brilliant idea, and as Tom had thought of it, he was elected to do it. He sneaked over the bridge, dodged from tree to tree, and went under the caravan. The steps were moved to one side, and he crept back to his friends. With this part of the mission accomplished they collected apples from the orchard and went back to the bridge. When they threw the apples at the caravan the result was immediate and quite spectacular. The door banged open and out flew Albert Bush. Flying is what he was doing because he did not notice the steps had been removed. But it was not for long. He crashed to the floor with a howl. He could not have been hurt much because with one bound he was up and running towards them. They scattered. Timmy ran along the hedge for a bit and then jumped in; the others ran in all directions. After a while Albert Bush came limping back across the orchard; he was alone, so obviously he had not caught any of the boys. Trying hard to contain his persistent cough, Timmy peered out from between the leaves. To his horror it looked as if Albert Bush was coming straight towards his hiding place. Maybe he's seen me, thought Timmy with rising terror, but to his great relief, Albert Bush walked on by, muttering and talking to himself. "What a fierce looking old man," thought Timmy. "I wouldn't like him to catch me." There was a scraping sound as the old man pulled the steps back into place and then the door slammed. Timmy hoped Albert Bush was now safely in his caravan, but he waited a while to make sure the coast was clear, then crept out of his hiding place and set off for home.

It was Monday and Miss Madwit, the headmistress, was addressing the Morning Assembly. "I have had a very serious complaint from Mr Albert Bush. It appears there are some foolish children among you. Someone threw apples at his caravan and when he came out to investigate he fell from the door because the steps had been moved." She glared at them angrily. "This was a stupid thing to do. Mr Bush could have broken a leg or even worse, and I want the culprits to own up!" No hands were raised. "All right," said Miss Madwit, "I will give you until dinner time. If the culprits have not come forward by then there will not be any playtime." The culprits did not come forward. The children were really annoyed to lose their playtime. The next morning it was a gloomy assembly. Miss Madwit said that as the culprits would not own up playtime would be forfeited again and she would be writing to all their parents.

Timmy gasped when Tom put his hand up; was Tom going to confess?

"Please Miss," said Tom, all eyes on him. Miss Madwit stood up again; she thought he would have something to do with it.

"Yes Thomas." She said sternly. Tom took a deep breath.

"Please Miss, some of the children at the top of the village go to Parbrook school, and we have heard it's them." A small smile came on Miss Madwit's face. "Yes," she said thoughtfully, "you could well be right. I will tell Mr Bush the result of my investigations. My children would never do anything so stupid, and if they did they would own up." Tom was the hero of the day, and as he said when the four conspirators were on their own.

"I really fooled Miss Dimwit today, didn't I?"

But the lure of the plums was great, and a few days later found Tom and Timmy at the bridge overlooking the plum trees and the caravan. They had provided themselves with an alibi, telling all that they were going fishing. As soon as they were out of sight the fishing rods were hidden, then via back lanes and over fields they arrived at the bridge without seeing anyone. It was a different plan this time. The plank that served as a bridge was pulled over, so it was only just balanced on the far side. If they were chased by Albert Bush, he and the plank would fall in the ditch; he would not break a leg, or worse, as Miss Madwit had feared, but only get wet or muddy. Apples were thrown at the caravan, but there was no response, so Albert Bush was out. The next part of the plan was put into action. They went back along the hedge, through a small gap that had been found earlier, jumped the ditch and back to the plum trees. The bridge was left as it was so that if Albert Bush came back there would be plenty of warning, as he fell in the ditch. But the plums were not fully ripe. Although they were disappointed a few were almost edible, so they filled their pockets and left through the small gap. It was almost time for tea so they headed for home. The plums made good catapult ammunition even if they were not much good for eating.

"They'll be ripe in a week or two," said Tom. "Then we shall try again." The boy's were at Tom's gate making plans for the next day, when Timmy suddenly thought about the way they had left the old man's bridge.

"He'll fall in the ditch!" he exclaimed.

"Well I'm blowed, I'm not going back to fix it now," said Tom. "Neither am I," replied Timmy. "He's probably found it by now anyway and not only that my tea should be ready so I'm going home." This he did and promptly forgot all about the bridge.

A couple of weeks later found Timmy and his mother a long way from home. They were going to a hospital for Timmy to have a chest X-ray. It had been a long journey because it was not in the nearest town, but one further away. The buses did not connect very well, so it was an all day excursion. From the reception they were directed to another part of the hospital and, after talking to someone in a cubby hole, on to the waiting room. When they walked into the waiting room Timmy could not believe his eyes. There was Albert Bush, his foot in plaster, and crutches leaning against the chair. He tried to hide behind his mother, but, to his dismay, she knew him.

"What a surprise to see you here Mr Bush," she said. "What have you been up to?"

"They think I have a broken bone in my foot," he said.

"Oh and how did you do that?" asked his mother.

"On my bridge; fell in the ditch," he said gruffly, huge staring eyes glaring at Timmy. Timmy felt his face burning, his legs felt weak and he started to shake so much he had to sit down. He grabbed a magazine and buried his head in it. His mother and Albert Bush started to talk about things in general and gossip from the village. He tried not to listen, but his head snapped up from the magazine when he heard Albert Bush say. "Do you like plums, Mrs Richards?"

"Well yes I do," replied his mother. "Then send that young'un up with a basket tomorrow," he said glaring at Timmy again. While the two adults were talking, it now seemed to Timmy, that Albert Bush was staring at him all the time. It was a great relief when they were called into the X-ray room. When they came out Albert Bush had gone; thank goodness for that thought Timmy, the feeling of relief returning. He had been dreading going back into the waiting room. On the bus going home his mother said, "It was nice of Albert Bush to offer us some plums. He is a gruff old man though. He's not like any of the other Bush families that live in the village."

Timmy turned from staring out of the window.

"Dad said there are so many Bushes in the village, if there was one more you could make a B---- great hedge."

For this he got a cuff around the head.

"But Dad said it," cried Timmy.

"You should not repeat what others say, and I shall be having a word with your father when we get home." his mother said angrily.

For the rest of the journey they travelled in almost silence, each with their own thoughts. Timmy was trying hard to think of a way he could dodge going for the plums the next day. But try as he might he could not think of a plan that would save him; he was sure Albert Bush knew he was responsible for the bridge.

When he got up in the morning it was bright and sunny. Timmy had hoped it would be raining so he would not be able to go out. There on the kitchen table beside his breakfast was the basket. He took such a long time over his breakfast his mother told him off, she wanted to clear up. At last he had finished, she put the basket in his hand and almost had to push him out of the door. He dawdled up through the village. He talked to old ladies, stroked cats, patted dogs and even talked to two cows overlooking a gate, but all too fast he found himself at the bridge. The bridge had changed; it was now a proper bridge, three or four planks wide with railings along one side. He hung about the bridge for a long time, not daring to go over it and knock on the caravan door. It was then he had an idea. He would tell his mother Albert Bush was out; and this is what he did, but it was all to no avail because his mother sent him up again after dinner. So it was he found himself at the bridge once again. His attention was taken with a buzzard circling overhead with two crows mobbing it. His mind was a long way off as he watched these birds wheeling above, so when a loud gruff voice from behind said, "Now then young'un." He almost jumped out of his skin. "Heh Heh Heh," cackled Albert Bush. "Did I frighten you?" Timmy turned to look at him. Could that grimace really be a smile? If so, it made his face look even worse than usual.

"Go on then, over the bridge. Let's find you a ladder to get the plums," said Albert Bush sounding almost friendly. He hobbled over to a ramshackle shed. To open the door he had to move a plank of wood that was almost broken in half, as he threw it to one side he turned to Timmy and said, "That used to be my bridge."

"But it's broken, "said Timmy.

"Well, of course it is, that's why I've got a new bridge."

"So the bridge didn't slide in the ditch because it was on the edge, it just broke?" said Timmy. "Of course it broke, it was rotten, that's how I hurt my foot you stupid boy. It had somehow moved and I put it back in position and jumped on it, to make sure it was safe and it broke." Timmy grabbed the ladder, ran over to the first tree; put the ladder against a branch and climbed up. A great cloud had lifted and his heart felt light. He and Tom were not responsible for Albert Bush's broken foot; the silly old man had jumped up and down on the bridge and the wood was rotten. He picked as fast as he could, everything that came to hand. Old plums, green plums, rotten plums, twigs, leaves, the lot. He threw the ladder in the shed and shouted goodbye to Albert Bush, who looked out of the window and said, "Don't forget to tell your mother she owes me sixpence for the plums." Timmy felt he was floating on air as he skipped down through the village; a great weight had been lifted off his shoulders. He dumped the basket on the table, and shouted to his mother.

"The plums are on the table Mum; you owe Albert Bush a tanner for them."

"The old skinflint," she said as she came down the

stairs, "He did not say I would have to pay for them." Then she saw the basket of old plums, green plums, rotten plums, twigs, and leaves on the table.

"Timmy," she said, "did you or Albert Bush pick these? Timmy, Timmy, where are you?" But Timmy had gone out, looking for the next adventure.

The Marquee

"That was a good story, Granddad." Said Stuart, "But what was wrong with Timmy? Tom said Timmy could not run very far and he wasn't even allowed to ride his bike. Was he ill?"

"Yes he was," said the old man. "The results of the X-rays came through on the following Friday and they were not good."

It was a sombre meeting in the doctor's surgery on that Friday morning. The doctor; a kindly man who had been the family doctor for as long as Timmy could remember; examined the X-ray negatives for a long time. He held them up to the light from the window turning them this way and that way, there was much dooting, frowning and shaking of the head. He then turned to Timmy's mother and said, "This does not look good at all, Mrs Richards." He looked at Timmy over the top of his horn-rimmed glasses.

"Take your clothes off young man, and let's give you another thorough examination."

Timmy took off his clothes; he was as skinny as the proverbial rake, there was not an ounce of meat on him.

"He has always been thin," said his mother to a comment made by the doctor. "Heaven knows why, he eats enough for two."

Timmy felt the cold stethoscope all over his body and there was much tapping and poking. He did not know what was wrong with him but he knew it must be something serious. Telling Timmy to get dressed, the doctor turned back to his mother and said, "You must take this boy home and put him to bed immediately."

Timmy's face began to crumble. With tears welling in his eyes, he looked imploringly at his mother.

"But it's the fête tomorrow, Mum," he wailed.

"I know Timmy, love," she said; she too now had tears in her eyes. "Doctor can't we let him go to the fête and then put him to bed? As you know, our house is opposite the show ground; the window in Timmy's bedroom actually overlooks it. How can I not let him go?"

"I can only advise you professionally, Mrs Richards," replied the Doctor. "The sooner he gets proper rest, the better."

His mother kept him indoors for the remainder of the day and when his father came home from work they decided he could go to the fête following day.

"Thanks Mum, thanks Dad," said Timmy. "Can I go out now and talk to my friends."

"OK," they said. "You must take it very easy though, no running about or anything strenuous. Do you understand that?"

"I do," said Timmy as put his coat on. But it was a complete waste of time telling Timmy anything like that.

The annual fête was one of the highlights in the village calendar and included a Flower Show and Gymkhana. On the day before the Flower Show a large marquee was erected, this year it seemed especially big, having four poles. They were told by the people that erected the tent and by their parents they must not play in it, but you might as well have told the sun to stop shining or the grass to stop growing. That evening found them playing in that big tent. Timmy was a very good climber and was the only one who could get right to the top of one of the poles. Then they played Cowboys and Indians, Tom

119

was Chief Sitting Bull, Rosemary was his squaw and John was a medicine man. That left Timmy as the only cowboy, but he of course had guns. After a while Tom shouted, "Stop. We're going to capture you Timmy."

"You can't, I'll shoot you," said Timmy. "You can't shoot us because you haven't got any bullets left," replied Tom. "You have only got two guns and you've fired twelve shots, I counted them and you haven't reloaded, so we're capturing you." So they did and tied him to the Totem Pole, well, tent post really. They soon tired of doing a war dance around him, but Timmy got worried when the squaw started to collect paper and sticks to burn him at the stake. He was now trying to get out of his bonds, and was very relieved when Sitting Bull said, "Indians do not burn pale faces at the stake." Anyway, they didn't have any matches. It was then there was a loud crack when the end tent post broke about a quarter of the way up. The top

three quarters of the post landed with a thud on the grass and then the canvass billowing like a parachute came slowly down around it. The Indians screaming and shouting; scrambled out of the marquee as fast as they could, leaving their prisoner tied to the pole next to the one that had just broken. Timmy was also screaming for he was now seriously panicking; but thankfully his fervent struggling resulted in him managing to loosen his bonds. He had just managed to free himself and was rubbing his wrists where the string had cut into them when, with a loud bang, the pole he had been tied to also broke. This was probably caused by the strain of the first pole breaking. Panicking again, Timmy shot to the far end of the marquee and had great difficulty lifting the side up so he could get out. At last he was out and he sat down on the grass panting and gasping for breath. He had made himself more tired than he had realised when he had climbed the tent pole and with the panic and struggle to free himself now felt rather weak. There was a lot of noise and commotion coming from the wrecked end of the marquee including grown up voices, and a lot of shouting. He decided he would not go round to that end as he was bound to get the blame for the marquee falling down, so instead he went through the hedge and along the back of the houses, then over the wall into his back garden. The light was on in the front room, peeping through the window he saw there was only one of his older sisters in. He crept in the back door and up the stairs and went to bed. Meanwhile back at the Marquee they were looking for him. Someone had gone to his house to see if he had gone home, but of course his sister had not seen him, another person had fetched his parents from the whist drive and all were searching for him. When they had crawled under the canvass and found the string still attached to the broken post Rosemary suggested he had gone to heaven, but, his father did not think so. His parents went back to the house just in case he had gone since they had arrived on the scene. They found him fast asleep in bed and woke him up. His father was furious.

"It wasn't my fault the tent fell down, Dad," he said sleepily.

"You must have done something," shouted his dad. "You never go to bed unless you're told." his mother said. "We'll deal with it tomorrow." As she closed the door she said to his father, "Go easy on him you know he's ill." And indeed he was. After the fête he was confined to bed, a whole new chapter was starting in his short life.

Interned

Timmy had a lovely day at the fête. What he liked most was the small travelling fair, he did not have much money for the rides, but he liked the music and watching the bumper cars gave him a thrill. One or two people even let him ride with them. When tired of the fair he watched the Gymkhana; he knew he would have to make the most of today because he was dreading the future and tried not to think about it.

After tea that evening he was confined to bed. Oh how he hated it. As the long days turned into weeks he grew listless and melancholy. A deep depression set in that was to last for many months and it was several months after that before it lifted completely.

Eventually it was decided he must be hospitalised. His parents knew this all along but had decided not to tell him until they had to; it seemed there was not a vacancy for him earlier. On the day he was scheduled to leave home, his mother dressed him to await the transport. She sat him in her chair which was in the corner of the kitchen, next to the Rayburn. She had not seen Timmy dressed for a long time and her heart went out to him. He was such a pathetic little creature; he seemed to have shrunk in the last few months. He sat there listless, eyes not focusing on anything, he probably would have been motionless had it not been for his incessant cough. This cough seemed to permeate the whole building and the house would be strangely quiet when he had gone.

It was late in the afternoon when a taxi came for him. The taxi was accompanied by an old nurse who came in to the house to speak to his mother and get her signature on a few forms. Her arrival in their house seemed to stir Timmy a bit and even in his listless state he thought she looked just like Popeye.

"Is he clean?" said the nurse to his mother as if Timmy was not there. "What do you mean, is he clean?" replied his mother. "Does he wet the bed?"

"No I don't!" snapped Timmy, staring at the nurse with his eyes blazing: but the truth is it had happened once or twice just lately, much to his embarrassment. His mother looked at him in surprise; it was the first time he had shown a spark of the old Timmy in a long while. This small encounter seemed to set the relationship between Timmy and the nurse for the whole of his stay in the hospital.

When they arrived at the hospital it was almost dark so Timmy could not see what the building looked like; not that he would have taken much interest even if it had been bright sunlight, because he had sunk back into his torpor. The taxi pulled round to the rear of the hospital and stopped on a small gravelled area; with the engine still running the driver helped them out of the car and drove off immediately. When the vehicle had gone they were left in almost total darkness; which did not seem to worry the nurse at all.

Clutching his small case and occasionally stumbling, he followed the sound of the crunching gravel under her feet, as she unerringly made her way towards a small door and opened it, revealing the dimly lit interior. In a cold flagstone room, he was told to sit on one of the benches which were tucked under several rough wooden tables. Although he didn't realise it at the time, this was the patient's dining room. He was given bread and butter with a mug of milk and then taken upstairs and along a corridor with many open doors on each side. They went through one of these and he was shown to his bed in a silent, dim room. The only source of light was filtering through the open doorway from a single bare bulb which hung half

way along the lengthy corridor they had just traversed. It seemed a very spartan room containing five beds and very little else; the wide open windows did not have any curtains and the door was missing from the frame. As soon as the nurse had gone the occupants of the other beds started to talk. They seemed younger than Timmy, some of them much younger.

"It's a pity, you've just missed visiting day," said one.

"Makes no difference, there'll be others," said Timmy, moodily.

"I've been here six visiting days," said the boy in the far corner.

"I've been here four," said another, the others volunteered they'd been here three and five. "How often was visiting days"? Timmy wanted to know, assuming they would be once or twice a week.

"Last Saturday in every month," was the reply. "Last Saturday in every month." Timmy mused to himself several times as he digested this information. It took a long time to sink in through his torpor but when it did he realised that these children had been here between three and six months. Suddenly he was devastated. His family doctor had said he would be in hospital between three and six weeks. Why should his stay be any different to the other children? Oh, why did grown-ups have to tell lies?

The top third of Timmy's bed was in a corner and the bottom stuck out in front of a large bay window. He turned to face the wall and he wept; great heaving sobs wracked his thin body. The other children became quiet, it is not known if their silence was for sympathy or they were just embarrassed by this older boy crying.

And how Timmy cried. Great heaving sobs wracked his thin body. He cried for the lies he had been told, he cried for his lost freedom, he cried because he was oh so sorry for himself, he cried, though he did not realise it, because of this seemingly all consuming deep depression. Not a nurse or anyone else looked in that room while Timmy wept and in the end he cried himself to sleep. Timmy only cried a few more times in his long stay at this hospital. Once when he woke from a nightmare, he had quite a few of these, and once when he had a particularly vivid dream of home and woke to find himself, in what was by then, the very familiar bleak surroundings.

In the morning his eyes bleary from the crying of the night before, Timmy watched in astonishment as the other children pulled the bedclothes off their beds and started to turn their mattresses over. This was no mean feat as some of those children were very small indeed. The old nurse came in and showed him what to do. The bedclothes had to be exact. There had to be proper corners and the blankets had to be exactly the same height from the floor on each side. The turnback on the hems had to be the correct side so that when the sheets and blankets were turned down they could not be seen. Many a bed was stripped and the clothes thrown on the floor just because the turnback on a hem was on the wrong side. When the culprit came back from breakfast, the bed would then have to be remade from scratch.

The toilet and wash room were downstairs and after that it was back to bed for Timmy. It was surprising they called this complete rest, because after all this exertion, Timmy was so tired he was almost asleep by the time breakfast came round; in fact some times he actually was. While the others had their breakfast in the dining room, he had his two pieces of cold bacon, a slice of cold fried bread and a mug of warm milk; sat up in bed. This was the set breakfast for every other day, on the alternative days it was porridge. Timmy didn't know which of these two depressing breakfasts were the worst, at least the porridge had the last vestige of warmth when it arrived; but it was sticky and lumpy. This boring diet was alleviated once a month by the inclusion of an egg.

With the exception of one other new inmate, the other children were allowed up for a varying amount of time each day. Most of them attended a small school attached to the hospital. The hospital itself was a farmhouse with all the interior doors removed and with windows that probably couldn't be shut, because they were always open. It was located in a beautiful setting, being the last building but one in a village at the end of a dead end valley in the Mendip Hills. Timmy was only allowed to sit up for his meals and the time dragged by endlessly. After a few days the elderly school teacher gave him a bit of work to do. This he could do lying on his stomach with a pillow under his chest, but he could not concentrate and was still very depressed; one day seemed to merge with the next.

As the weeks wore on a sense of anticipation seemed to grip the other children. The nearer it got to visiting day, the greater the anticipation. On the morning of the great day, the excitement was so great, some of it even got through to Timmy. For the visit he was moved to another room. He didn't know why because it was just as bleak as the old room, only bigger. Because of the distance and the complexity of their journey his parents were not expected until after lunch. He was allowed to sit up on this day so he observed the distressing scenes happening all around him. In most cases the early excitement and laughter gave way to tears as the visits came near to the end. Then the crying and the begging to be taken home left many parents in anguish. There were not many dry eyes as visitors left that hospital. Timmy felt detached from these events, as if he was above looking down on that room, and the tableau's unfolding before him. He made a conscious decision he would not put his parents or himself through that sort of trauma. When they arrived he was very quiet, but he answered their questions and read his favourite comics they had bought him. Comics were not allowed in this hospital so the visitors had to take them away again. His parents found it very difficult to have a conversation with him. Timmy for his part was glad to see them, but he was still depressed and offered very little, only answering their queries.

The visit was not a great success and this seemed to set the pattern for the next two or three. It might have been better if he had let himself go as the other children had. For his parents and the other visitors it grew increasingly more uncomfortable as the winter drew near. Bright red winter overblankets were placed on all the beds and this seemed to cheer those dull rooms up a bit, but without heating, doors and windows that never closed; there were a lot of cold people on those last Saturdays in every month. The inmates, to a certain extent, grew accustomed to these conditions.

One morning about a month before Christmas, Timmy

woke to find he could hardly move his legs. He could not feel any pain, it just felt as if there was a great weight on them. He looked out over his bedclothes in a rising panic, and to his astonishment he could see why. Where the lower part of his bed stuck out in front of the window it was covered by a huge pile of snow. Timmy was fascinated. This will be something to tell Tom when I get out, he thought. He jumped out of bed and started to make a snowman on it, only to be severely reprimanded by the nurse, when she came in. But, whereas before there only seemed to be dullness; now there was a bit of a spark in him. Timmy was at last getting better.

As his health slowly returned Timmy started to take more of an interest in his surroundings and he began to realise what a hard, even harsh, regime reigned in this establishment. It was dominated by the only two qualified nursing staff, the Matron and the old nurse. Most of the other staff involved in the running of this small hospital, were dailies from the village. There were one or two who lived in but they did not seem to stay for long. Timmy found most of these auxiliary staff OK, but they did not seem have much influence.

The elderly teacher did have influence and she was later, to become his friend, providing him with many books as he was now becoming an avid reader. Before he was halfway through his stay he had read all the suitable books in the small library, so the additional she lent him were really appreciated. By Christmas, Timmy was allowed up for a few hours a day. This was great, he was feeling good. The depression had completely gone. He was given shorts, a shirt, underpants and that was it. These were changed once a week. Woe betide the child whose underwear was soiled in the slightest way. No shoes or socks were worn; it is surprising how quickly feet harden and how cumbersome shoes felt on the few occasions when they were worn.

Although he missed his freedom, things were better for Timmy. He attended the school in his short time away from the bed, here he was in for another surprise. There was hardly any furniture. There were cupboards and shelves around the sides, but there were not any desks or chairs. Children had to do their school work lying face down on the floor. The theory was, this would expand the chest; whether it worked or not who knows. In the Schoolroom they did a play for their visitors. This seemed to be a great success and there were a lot of tears in the audience, though they of course, were prejudiced. It was decided to do it again for the villagers in the New Year.

Christmas came and went very quietly, there being only six or seven patients, the others having been allowed home. A few months later Timmy could hardly remember any of it. The only thing that stuck in his mind was the bubble pipe. One of the patients had received a pipe for making bubbles as a Christmas present, and Timmy had persuaded the old nurse to put it in her mouth. The portrayal of Popeye was complete. But he did remember the snow; there was a lot of it that year. His greatest pleasure was the sledge. It was huge and would hold up to twelve children at a squash. For its size it was fairly light and given the right sort of snow would glide down even a very slight incline. On the sloping field at the back of the hospital it was great fun. The sledge had been given to the hospital by the army. Timmy would have loved to take it home, it was so much better than the homemade toboggans he and his mates had used the year before.

Two months into the New Year, and Timmy was allowed up all day. He didn't mind the school work during the week, but what he really liked was the walks on the hills at the weekends. The terrain was so different to the countryside of his home. Tom would like it up here he thought. Whenever he thought of home and Tom, and his other friends it was like thinking of another life.

One windy day high on the hills, Timmy's thoughts were confirmed; he was not thinking of home, but of the Matron. She was quite mad. He had thought she was mad all along, but now he was quite sure. At her behest, the sledge had been dragged to the top of the hills; Timmy had assumed there would be some long meandering way down and it would be great ride. But he was wrong. She wanted to go straight down the way they had come up. When they had come up they had zigzagged, using old drover's trails and sheep paths because it was so steep, in some places it was almost forty-five degrees. There were gorse bushes, brambles, gullies and at the bottom, a hedge dividing the hills from the fields. How could anyone contemplate tobogganing down that hill? Even if the sledge reached the bottom, the only way it could stop would be by hitting the hedge.

"You're not frightened, are you Timmy?" said the Matron.

"Of course he's not frightened," said one of the other children. "Timmy's not frightened of anything. Are you Timmy?" Timmy did not answer.

"Come on, Timmy, you can sit in the front," said one of the others. "We know that's what you want." He had to do it; he could not lose face, even though he was scared stiff. He had become the unofficial leader, being one of the eldest and he had been in the hospital longer than most. In the evenings he would often tell stories from the books he had read, but mostly it was tales of himself and his great mate, Tom. When telling of these exploits and adventures he would of course always be the hero, so it was not surprising these younger children thought he was not frightened of anything.

As for the Matron, she was the King or Queen of her domain and whatever she said or wanted, was acted on by patients and staff alike, with no question asked. It was not surprising the children were not worried about going down the hill on the sledge; if the Matron said it was all right, then it had to be all right. Timmy had been amazed by some of the things she had said and done. Now she was trying to kill them and just to save face, he was going along with it. And so the sledge set off, with seven squealing and laughing children in the middle of the vehicle, one large woman sitting at the back, a dog running around barking, and Timmy almost rigid with fear, holding the reins at the front. The sledge quickly picked up speed and Buster the dog was soon left behind. They had not gone very far when one runner went over a gorse bush, tipping the sledge over. This had the effect of scattering the occupants all down the hill, the sledge now upside down, went a bit further and came to a rest on another bush. Miraculously no one was hurt. Timmy was quite relieved they had got away with it so lightly. It was then he realised just how mad this Matron was, she had them drag the sledge back up to the top to have another go. She realigned the sledge slightly to miss the first offending bush and off they set again.

This time they really picked up speed, Timmy could feel the wind in his face as tall grasses and brambles thrashed by. The sledge then hit a group of small gorse bushes and brambles; this had the effect of jolting Timmy off the front, but the sledge kept going and went right over the top of him. When the sledge had passed Timmy looked up gingerly. He had landed face down and was looking straight down the hill. He did not think he was hurt, the bushes were quite springy but his knees felt sore where the brambles and prickles had been rammed in. This was later to give him some trouble as each little prick and scratch turned septic. Strangely the sledge was nowhere to be seen, and except for the wind, it was very quiet.

Suddenly the sledge appeared out of a hollow, travelling really fast, only to disappear again into another dip. When it reappeared the powdery snow was coming up from the rear, looking almost like smoke, so much so that Timmy had a job to see exactly what happened next. He watched almost mesmerised; the sledge was not going straight down now, but was now proceeding at an angle, though it was still going to hit the hedge. Suddenly it seemed to flip over and flew high in the air, bodies going everywhere. Timmy got up and ran stumbling and slipping down towards them, he feared the worst. Oh why hadn't he tried to stop that crazy woman? If he thought the first time had been a miracle, this was a double one. Not one person was hurt. The sledge had turned over just before the deep snow that had accumulated between the hillside and the hedge and this is what they had all landed in. The sledge was high in the hedge and they could not even reach it let alone rescue it. Timmy was pleased about that, because if they had managed to rescue it he was quite sure, the Matron would want to go back up the hill and have another go.

Timmy was sorry to see the snow had gone next morning, but as they had to go to school it did not matter a lot. Anyway, the sledge was stuck in a hedge and it was several days before the gardener rescued it and did some minor repairs; so it was ready when there was another fall about halfway through the week. The only trouble was it was snowing too hard for them to go out before tea and afterwards it was too dark. When they had to go to bed

Timmy and another boy stood in the window looking out at an almost magical scene. The snow had stopped and there was a full moon, it was almost as bright as daylight.

"Wouldn't it be nice to go tobogganing now, in the moonlight," said the boy. "Why don' we do it then?" said Timmy. "We could creep out when all the others are asleep. Matron and the nurse's rooms are at the front of the house, it's only the new lady this side, and she's in one of the attic rooms. We could get out through those small windows in the wash room; I think they could be reached if we stand on the sinks."

"Oh yes!" said the boy; He was a little in awe of Timmy. "It would be an adventure, almost like the ones you and Tom used to have." And so they went to bed and pretended to be asleep, only in Timmy's case he actually went to sleep. The other boy had to wake him up when he thought it was time to go.

"I don't know how you can sleep, Timmy," he said. "I've been so excited, I'm now almost shaking. But then, you're used to this sort of thing aren't you?" Timmy didn't say anything; he hadn't meant to go to sleep, in fact he had tried hard to stay awake, but he seemed to be very tired. They put clothes on over their pyjamas and crept out onto the landing as quietly as possible, not a sound was made when passing the Matron's rooms because the slightest noise would start Buster barking. Then on through the big room where there were about ten occupied beds and down the stairs they crept, hearts pounding.

It was easier than expected, to get out through the small windows in the wash room, but it was a big drop on the outside. There was a severe frost and when walking Timmy felt a very satisfying crunch underfoot. The sledge was taken from the shed and they headed for the far side of the field. There was a row of Elm trees in the hedge on this side. The theory was that they would walk up the field under the trees so that if anyone looked out of a window, they would not be seen in the shade. It was a good job the theory was not put to the test, because even in the shade, it was very light, with the bright moonlight reflecting off the snow.

When they got to the top they were puffed out; normally there were a lot of children pulling or pushing the sledge, for two it was quite a struggle. They turned it around and prepared to descend. The scene was breathtaking, the air was crystal clear and the view seemed to go on forever. They pushed the sledge and jumped on. It was a big field, not particularly steep, but a good speed could be achieved before it levelled out at the bottom. They both found it really exhilarating. For Timmy, this was the most beautiful thing he had ever done. The only sound was the hissing of the snow under the runners. As soon as the sledge came to a stand they turned it round and started to drag it back up. When they reached the top this time Timmy was whacked, it took him a long time to catch his breath before he was ready to go on the next fantastic trip. This time when they reached the bottom the sledge was put away in the shed and they made there way back to where they had left the windows open. The only trouble was the windows were too high to get back in.

"What we need is something to stand on," said Timmy. "I know, let's use the sledge, it would make a good ladder." So they retrieved the sledge from the shed and leant it against the wall. As Timmy had said it made a good ladder, but as they were crawling through the windows the sledge fell with a clatter. They could hear Buster barking and they froze half in and half out, they stayed in this position for ages waiting for the lights to come on. But they didn't and Buster stopped barking. After a while they finished crawling in, closed the windows and crept up to bed. In the morning the other children had to wake Timmy.

"Come on, Timmy," said one. "The snow hasn't gone so we can go on the sledge again today." Timmy got up and looked out of the window bleared-eyed through lack of sleep. He went back to his bed and started to dress. Suddenly his body stiffened as the realisation of the scene he had just witnessed sunk in. He jumped up and ran back to the window. There for all to see was the evidence of their escapade of night before. Sledge trails the whole length of the field. The nurse and others came into the room, but did not seem to notice the sledge lines in the snow, or if they did, the implications were not realised. Timmy was on tender hooks as he made his bed, washed and went to breakfast. Any minute he was expecting someone to burst in and demand to know who had been tobogganing overnight. He bolted his food down and as soon as they would let him, rushed outside. There was normally only a few minutes between breakfast and school. The gardener was coming in as Timmy burst out and they collided. After they had sorted themselves out, the gardener asked Timmy if the Matron was in the dining room.

"No," said Timmy, "I saw her going out in the car."

"Humph," said the gardener. "I was going to report the misuse of the sledge." Timmy's heart would have sunk to his boots, if he had been wearing any. "I was going to tell her not to let you use it again," continued the gardener. "It was left on the path and when trying to get passed it, I slipped over."

"I'm ever so sorry," said Timmy. "I promise we will put it away as soon as we finish with it, from now on."

"Just you make sure you do then," muttered the

gardener, as he clumped back up the path. Timmy gave a huge sigh of relief. He collected as many children as he could. Some of them he told to put the sledge away. All of the others he took up to the field and had them scuff the snow and generally run about; hopefully this would obliterate the sledge trails. As the others came out from breakfast, they joined in, they didn't know why they were doing it, but it was good fun. The teacher came out to ring the handbell, but the sight she saw stopped her in her tracks. Everyone was now helping Timmy, they were strung out in a rough line, running, scuffing, and jumping about in the snow, the whole length of the field. It did look strange. She rang the bell and when the first of them came down she asked what they were doing.

"It's a new game that Timmy's made up," she was told. Timmy was about the last to come down out of the field.

"What is this new game then, Timmy?" She asked.

"It's not a new game Miss," said Jimmy. "It's for the public play we're doing this evening. I want it to look as if lots and lots of people have come to see it."

"That's nice, Timmy," said the teacher, but as she turned away there was a frown on her face. He is a strange boy sometimes she thought. The field only leads to the hills, so who is he pretending will be coming from that direction. As for Timmy he was thinking. That was a poor excuse, but it was all I could think of on the spur of the moment.

But Timmy was not to be in that play in the evening he was in for a bad shock.

"And that, young people is where we will have to finish; it's time to go to sleep," said the old man.

"Can't you tell us about the bad shock that Timmy was going to get, Granddad?" said James.

"No, we haven't got time," was the reply.

137

"OK," said Stuart, "but can you tell us what illness Timmy had? You never did say."

"It was Tuberculosis or TB for short. In many ways Timmy and his fellow patients were lucky, they were the early recipients of a new drug from America. Without it Timmy's chances of making a complete recovery would not have been very good."

Interned (Part 2)

"We don't seem to be getting many bites, Granddad," said Stuart as they sat on the bank together. He was getting fed up with peering at a red float which had not moved for ages. "Are you sure there are any fish in this river?"

"Oh yes," said the old man. "Or should I say there was plenty in the past; Tom and Timmy fished this river all the time and they caught lots of fish."

"Well, there does not seem to be many now, Granddad; maybe they caught them all." replied Stuart. "Talking of Tom and Timmy, why don't you finish off the story of Timmy's stay in the hospital?"

"OK," said the grandfather. "If that's what you want. I wonder if James would like to hear the rest of the story?"

"I'll go and find him. I bet he hasn't caught any fish either?" said Stuart, and with that off he went to look for his brother. He was quite right; James had not caught a thing and was now bored as he was, so a chance to listen to more of grandfather's tales was quite welcome. So once again they settled down on the riverbank to listen to tales of yesteryear.

The morning session of school was only about half an hour old when someone came for Timmy. He was told the doctor was waiting to see him in the main building. This was not a surprise for Timmy, having had an X-ray the previous week. It was quite often the case, X-ray one week, doctor examination sometime the next. He was shown into the Matrons study, this room was usually used by the visiting doctor. Quite surprisingly there were two doctors. He was told to strip off and they gave him a thorough examination, showing quite a lot of interest in his knees. The scratches and sores had not healed and most were now weeping. There was a lot of H'mms and Ah's and poking, listening, tapping and examining of the X-ray negatives. They then told him to get dressed and go into the next room and wait for the Matron. Timmy had never been in this room before. It smelt quite musty, the carpeted floor felt strange under his feet. There was a large mirror and Timmy looked at himself, he hadn't seen a mirror since he had been here. The boy looking back seemed to be a stranger, especially as the scratches on his face were as angry looking as those on his legs. He pulled faces at himself and was almost upside down when the Matron came in. Timmy jumped up.

"It's all right," she said, putting her hand on his shoulder. "But I'm afraid I have some bad news. You have to have complete rest, so it's back to bed again for you young man." To say he was devastated is an understatement in the extreme. Timmy walked up the stairs to his room in a daze, his legs and hands shaking. He had thought he would soon be going home, but after seven visiting days, almost eight long months, he was back where he started. But deep down and at the back of his mind, he knew there was something wrong and he knew he was not yet well. Undressing in front of the window he gazed out with misty eyes at that wonderful, wonderful, sight.

Oh how his heart ached as he looked at the snowy hills, towering above the field where he had been tobogganing only the night before. The morning sun was glistening on the wet branches of the big elm trees with the rooks wheeling above. He took all this in, because he knew he would not be going out of this building or even this room for a long time to come. Timmy tried not cry; he had promised himself that this place, these people, would not make him cry again. But there was something running down his face, he rubbed his cheeks angrily and climbed into bed. He couldn't even see the window from his bed let alone look out. Timmy tried not to cry, he said to himself, "They won't make me cry, I won't cry." But it wasn't long before he had to turn the pillow over because one side was so wet.

This time the deep depression he had experienced the first time around, did not set in. Instead he started to have nightmares. There were two distinctively different nightmares, each as terrifying as the other. He would feel a nightmare coming on, but seemed powerless to stop it. Sitting up seemed to keep it away for while, but it was still there in the back of his mind. In those dim unheated rooms with the windows open, it was too cold to sit up for long; so eventually he had to lie down. When he did so the nightmares seemed to be there waiting and would overwhelmed him. He would be found by one of the staff thrashing about and screaming, as if in some sort of fit. These nightly sessions left Timmy feeling confused and tired. He seemed to be sleeping more in the day than at night. They left the light on in his room and this did seem to help a bit. It was complete rest this time, he didn't have to make his own bed and there was a cubicle in the corner with toilet facilities. The doctors thought his nightmares might be a side affect of the course of drugs, though they had not heard of this effect before and it had not happened to Timmy when he first came to the hospital. Their theory was probably correct, because as the drugs were reduced the nightmares became more sporadic and eventually ceased all together. It was not too long before he was moved back into the room with the other boys. The other children visited him as often as they could and kept him up to date with things that were happening and the hospital gossip. Visiting other children in bed was strictly forbidden and they risked severe reprimands if caught, and they quite often were. The staff blamed Timmy, but it was not his fault, he did try to tell the others not to come, though he really did like their company, on those long miserable days. But it was to no avail. The fact that they wanted to come and talk to him, even though they risked getting into trouble was not lost on Timmy. He felt rather humbled, especially as most of those who risked the wrath of the nursing staff, were some of the youngest children in the hospital.

He was now reading a great deal and the elderly teacher introduced him to many new books and authors. She spent a lot of her own time talking to him and an unlikely friendship formed. The staff seemed to have given up trying to stop the other children visiting him. With his reading and the daily visits from the teacher and the other inmates, the days went by much quicker this time, certainly better than when he was first bedridden.

There was a stir in the hospital; Timmy could almost physically feel it. There was a great sense of excitement that was running through the whole building; affecting both patients and staff alike. The carnival-like atmosphere was heightened by people running hither and thither, as they bustled to get themselves ready for this great day. In preparation for this famous day decorations and buntings had been put up in all the rooms; there were flags stuck in every conceivable location and pictures covered nearly all the walls. Timmy thought it all looked rather jolly. Though he had not taken any part in any of these preparations and he knew most of today's festivities would pass him by; he was not unhappy, having laughed at some of the antics of others as they decorated the rooms. Despite the knowledge that his involvement in much of the day's proceedings would be minimal, he also had a sense of anticipation. For today was the Queen's Coronation.

Timmy, as an onlooker, seemed to be the only person not taking part in all this activity. He was still supposed to be having complete rest; though with all this commotion, how could he rest? He sat himself up in bed and watched all the comings and goings with interest. They had moved him into the big room about a week ago, so that repair work could be done in his old room. From his new bed he had a commanding view of the long corridor. Along this corridor, there seemed to be turmoil and utter confusion as people went from room to room getting themselves ready and helping others to get ready in their best clothes. The hustle and bustle gradually subsided as individuals and groups of people made their way down to the front lawn, this being the assembly point.

When they had all gone, Timmy thought the place looked like a bomb had hit it, with boxes, paper, bits of clothing and other things all over the place. He could hear the hub-bub of voices and squeals of laughter from below his window as they waited for the off. The window was too high for Timmy to look out, but he overcame that by climbing on a small chest of drawers. He was just in time to see them set off in crocodile fashion down the long garden path. All the staff were in their best clothes, but it was the patients that caught Timmy's eye. The girls were in their dresses with shoes and socks, most wore ribbons or headbands in their hair; which to Timmy's eyes seemed to transform them. The boys for their part had on shirts, short trousers, shoes and socks and hair combed and kept in place with some sort of oil. 'They do look smart', he thought as they turned into the lane and went out of view; in some strange way he felt rather proud of them. They were going in to the village to watch the coronation on someone's television. How they were all going to watch it on one little television Timmy had no idea. He had seen a television once in a shop window; it had been when he and his mother had been visiting the local town for his X-ray, and he was not overly impressed. Timmy climbed down from the window and stood in the middle of the room. How quiet it was he thought, he had never known this hospital so quiet. He wondered if he was the only person in the building, if so it did not worry him. Solitude was one thing that was hard to find in this establishment, so he decided to make the most of it. The Matron's rooms had intrigued him ever since he had been here; only getting glimpses of the interior as she went in or out. So now was his chance to have a look in the Matron's rooms, and a few other places, patents were barred from. But he was in for a disappointment because the door was locked. As he stood in the corridor wondering what to do next, he realised how cold he was; in fact he was blooming freezing. He had got cold when hanging out of the window and now this draught in the corridor was blowing like a gale.

'I think I'll get into bed and warm up before I do anything else', he thought to himself. This is what he did, but in the act of warming up he fell asleep and the next thing he knew he was being woken by a clonking noise which seemed to get louder and louder. It was the children returning from the village and it was they who were making the clonking noise; as they clomped up the stairs and across the wooden floors in their unaccustomed shoes.

'Well that's an opportunity lost', thought Timmy. 'I shall never get a chance like that again to explore this place'. He promptly forgot all about his lost chances as he was regaled by the others on their day out, with cream buns and fizzy pop; the actual coronation seemed to take second place.

His treatment and the rest cure seemed to be working and it was a much brighter Timmy when a month or two later he was allowed to get up for a few hours each day. As the time went by and he started to get better he got into more scrapes, in fact the better he got, the escapades became more outrageous. It was at this time his parents unexpectedly bought Tom in to see him and WOW! He had long trousers.

The other children were really interested in Tom because of Timmy's stories, but for Timmy and Tom they felt rather awkward. They felt rather like strangers, both looked different to the memories they had of each other. Timmy thought Tom looked almost like a man. As for Timmy, although he had grown taller he was, if anything, thinner than when he had first gone into hospital. His short trousers were now too small for him and clomping about with unaccustomed shoes on the other end of his long skinny legs; he felt and looked rather clumsy, especially when compared with the sophisticated looking Tom. For Timmy this was extremely disappointing. He had dreamt of the day they would meet again and almost every day when he was doing something or getting into another scrape, he would think, 'I'll tell Tom about this', or, 'I wonder what Tom would have done'? Now they did not seem to be able to communicate properly. It could have been because his parents were there, but whatever the reason, Tom did not visit again. After this visit, whenever Timmy thought about Tom and it was not so often now, he felt a little confused and rather sad. The thought of Tom and the things and stories he had to tell him, had helped to keep him going through his long internment. Now he was not even sure if they would be friends when he got out.

His one long abiding friend in the hospital was the teacher. They seemed to enjoy each others company and he would tell her about his latest troubles. Normally it was on a Monday because things seemed to happen at the weekend. It would usually start with the Matron, or one of the other staff complaining to the teacher about something or the other he had done, this quite often before she had time to take her coat off, or sit down. They told her because there was an undoubted friendship between them and she seemed to have more influence over him than anyone else. She would ask the questions and he would solemnly tell her in detail about the latest escapade. One in particular she had him tell several times.

Sheep had been put in the large hospital field. This was done several times a year, it was a cheap way of keeping the grass down and the children liked them. One of these sheep was very tame.

"It's because it has been hand-reared," the man had said, when he and the dog had first put the sheep in the field. This tame sheep was very popular with the children and would follow them around begging titbits they saved from meals, or picked from the garden, when the gardener was not looking. At this time there had been a large influx of patients and as a result Timmy and two of the older boys had been moved into one of the attic rooms. They loved it. There was only one of the auxiliary staff living up here and she did not hang about the hospital for very long when she was not on duty. This meant for long periods of time they did not see anyone. The cleaner had normally come and gone while they were at school.

Timmy's old bed and the one opposite were supposed to be occupied by two small girls, but the staff could not get these sisters to stay in bed. For hours on end, they would gaze out of the window, watching the other children at play. They were supposed to have complete rest, but, the only way this could have been enforced, would have been to tie them to their beds. One day when Timmy was walking by their room, they called him in.

"We have heard you can do almost anything," the oldest one of them said. Timmy did not say anything, wondering what would come next.

"Can you fix it for us to stroke and pet that tame lamb, before they take it away?" She continued, in a rather babyish way of talking. Timmy looked at the small pretty faces and the two pairs of big pleading eyes. How could he refuse? He had never spoken to them before but his ego was such, that he heard himself say. "Yes I'll think of something, that should not be too difficult." A few minutes later as he was walking down the stairs, he was thinking to himself. "What on earth made me say that; how am I going to do it?"

With one or two others they put their minds to work on how Timmy's promise could be accomplished. There had been a lot of them to start with, but with some of the silly ideas and suggestions, most had left. They had left because they did not want to be involved in another of Timmy's wild schemes, it would probably go wrong, just as most of them had gone wrong. Many had learnt their lesson the hard way and had ended up in trouble, when teaming up with Timmy. They didn't mind listening to his stories but did not want to be part of them again. At last they came up with a simple plan, that on the face of it should work. They would entice the sheep out of the field and into the wash room. The girls could then say they were going to the toilet. The toilet being on the other side of the washroom.

The first thing to do was to entice the sheep from the

field, through the play area, where there were swings, sea-saw, sandpit and the likes. Through a couple of small gates, one of which was supposed to stop animals and down a path to the wash room; all this without being seen.

There was then a discussion about what food the sheep liked best. The theory was, with the right sort of titbits, the sheep would follow the carrier of the food anywhere. One said, 'carrots' the other said 'cabbages', Timmy's thoughts were for lettuce, but as he was the one who was raiding the garden, he would get whatever he could. Timmy had a successful raid, and came back with carrots and cabbages, he could not find any lettuce, but there were other things he had collected, some of which he did not know the names of and other things he had never even seen before.

Now the fun started. The sheep were grazing at the top of the field so when the boys turned up with their goodies, they were mobbed by all the sheep, not just the one they wanted. Try as they might they could not stop the others stealing the food. Their plan was not a secret among the remaining children, who were all lined along the fence watching. There was lots of cheering and laughter, also many unhelpful suggestions; it was the best show for a long time, they really thought it was hilarious. The three biggest boys were being chased all over the field by a flock of sheep. The three chastened heroes managed to get back over the fence, with some of their goods intact. Timmy pleaded with the other children to lend a hand and to his surprise, nearly all agreed. With all this help and Timmy as the organiser, they went back into the field.

Timmy told them they were now cowboy's, who were going to cut one steer out of a great herd. Most of the children thoroughly enjoyed themselves, though it took more effort than expected. There was much cheering when finally they got the one sheep they wanted, out of the flock and into the play area. Most of the children were utterly exhausted, but there was a great a sense of achievement; it was as if an important game had been won. The next surprising thing was the behaviour of the animals. The whole flock of sheep were now standing all along the fence. Twenty minutes earlier, the children had been standing all along this wire fence, watching the sheep and the boys; now the sheep were doing the same on their side of the fence. It looked as if they were wondering what those children would be up too next and why one of their number was in the play area. This one lone sheep did not seem to be very happy and was doing it's best to get back with the flock.

Another surprising thing was; nobody from the hospital, or any other of the staff had noticed the strange things going on outside. It took the effort of all the children to get that one lone sheep through the gates. Once they were on the other side, the three boys were on their own and with the much depleted stock of goodies, tried to entice the sheep down the path. Now that the sheep was away from the flock, it seemed a bit more friendly and with much pushing and coaxing all four finally arrived in the wash room. This was only just in time, because a few seconds later they heard voices from the outside. Someone was walking along the path from the other direction and if they continued, the three boys and the sheep would be discovered.

The washroom had a big outer door that was always open during the day, so if it was closed, it would cause suspicion. There was another door into the dining room and kitchen, but the cook was in there. The only other way was up the back stairs to the bedrooms. These stairs were very narrow, but this was the escape route they chose. The sheep was very reluctant, but the boy's were desperate and with much shoving, heaving and pushing, it arrived at the top, without making too much noise. While two of them remained with the sheep, giving it the last of the spoils from the garden, the other crept back down the stairs. The idea being, he would give the all clear, when it was safe, to bring the animal back down. But he soon came running back up.

"It's the Matron," he said, "she's talking to the gardener, but, if she decides to go to her rooms she will probably come this way."

"We might as well take the sheep along to the girls room," said Timmy, "when she's gone, we can take it back downstairs and our mission will be accomplished." They were lucky, there did not seem to be any of the nursing staff around. There were some workmen doing something in the bathroom, but they would not be going that far, the bathroom being the far end of the passage. Timmy crept along the passage and pushed the door closed when their backs were turned. When they arrived at the girls' room, there was squeals of delight, so much so the boy's had to hush them up for fear of attracting attention. The delight did not last very long, because the sheep was not as soft and fluffy as it had looked from the window. In fact it was rather muddy and when inside was rather smelly. Timmy had not noticed it outside, but even he thought it ponged a bit now.

Another problem was they had used all the titbits so there was nothing to feed it with. The sheep went immediately to the window and put it's front feet on the low ledge, so it could look out. From the open window it could see the rest of the flock, in the field below and that's where it wanted to be; so it started a pitiful bleating and baaing. The boys rushed over to the window, they thought it might jump out and the noise it was making was bound to attract attention. But they soon jumped back because it started to do it's business all over the floor. Then the girls started crying and the commotion brought the workmen into the room. They too, thought the animal was going to jump out of the window, just as the boy' had and went straight into their rescue act. They charged over to the window, one each side and tried to lift the sheep up bodily. The only trouble was they were wearing hobnailed boots, just as most workmen did in those days. With the shiny wooden floor made worse with the sheep's business they were soon slipping and sliding all over the place and it wasn't long before all three had crashed to the floor.

At this stage of Timmy's recital of the weekend's events, the teacher stopped him. She stood up and ruffled his hair. Timmy thought she had a grimace on her face. She put her hand on her stomach, turned and walked out of the school room. He thought, maybe she's not well, she's probably got wind. She came back in, but turned and went straight back out again. This time she walked around the whole school building before coming back in looking more composed. She sat down and sternly told him to carry on with his story.

'She's not ill, just mad with me', thought Timmy. 'She's been out there, trying to compose herself, so she doesn't fly into a rage'. Though he would be the first to admit, she had never lost her temper with him before despite the fact she would have had plenty of reasons. The strange thing was, almost the same thing happened again when she had him tell the same story at a later date.

So he continued with his version of events, which was considerably different to that of the Matron's.

When the two men and the animal had fallen over, it was the sheep that had got up first and ran out into the corridor; where it proceeded to run up and down bleating. The men were now sitting up, giving vent to their opinions of sheep, children and other things, in no uncertain manner, especially the one with the cut on his head. The girls were now almost hysterical. The boys ran out into the corridor after the sheep just as the Matron's door burst open. It was unfortunate timing, because the sheep was just passing and for its escape route it chose the large main stairs opposite.

Now sheep's legs are not made for shiny polished stairs taken at high speed, but this one seemed to go quite well, it had almost got to the bottom of the first flight

before it seemed to bundle over. On the landing between the two flights of stairs, there was a rather elegant table with some sort of china on it. Timmy thought this table could not have been much good, because the legs broke like balsa wood when the sheep slid into it. The animal got up and seemed to shake itself, bits of wood and china flying all over the place. It then made for the second flight, these it descended without any more problems. The Matron almost flew down the stairs, but she was not quick enough, because there was a lot of crashing and shouting, the panicky sheep must have gone into the kitchen.

The boys had stayed at the top looking over the banisters, they had not given chase because the were not allowed to use the main stairs and they were certainly not allowed in the kitchen, in fact, Timmy had never even been in the kitchen. With the exception of a few sobs from the girls room and the low mutterings of the workmen it was now very quiet. The boys knew that the repercussions would soon begin. It was a sombre trio that trooped up to the attic room to await the outcome.

"It wasn't really our fault Miss," said Timmy to his teacher. "Things just seemed to go wrong. I don't like sheep anymore. They are not very bright, in fact, I think they're stupid. If it hadn't been for those clumsy workmen, the girls crying and that daft animal everything would have been all right. Now I have detention again and I'm being kept in while the others go to see a film."

He only told the teacher when he was caught, in some act or the other deemed wrong by the staff. To Timmy almost everything he did or wanted to do, was against the rules or was prohibited. He thought, maybe unjustly, the staff just wanted to keep the children in their place, so that a quiet time could be had by all. There did not seem to be any room for tenderness in this authoritarian regime. When thinking of home and the freedom he had enjoyed, it sometimes brought a lump to his throat. He would remember his mother saying, 'Here comes the lodger, he must be hungry', when he came straggling home, after being out all day. So he was caught often and it seemed to Timmy he would be telling the teacher another sorry episode almost every Monday. Like the time they tried to make a parachute out of a bed sheet, with a chair as a weight.

It was a very windy night when they made the

parachute and threw it over the low parapet outside of the attic window. An extra strong puff of wind came just at the wrong time and the back of the chair came off. The chair plunged to the ground and smashed, but the bed sheet with the back of the chair still tied to it, went up over the roof and out of sight. Timmy went down the stairs, climbing out of the now very familiar exit over the wash basins. He collected the bits and hid them under a bush. 'It's just as well the chair did break', he thought. 'If it had been whole I would never have got it though those small windows'. After the debacle with the sledge they had devised an efficient way of getting back into the hospital. Each night, empty milk crates were stacked outside the back door, to be collected by the milkman in the morning. These milk crates made great steps; though you had to be careful when moving them, as the slightest knock would make them rattle, and this noise almost always made Buster bark. Much to Timmy's surprise, no one ever did query why the crates had been moved. It could be that the milkman picked them up from wherever they were stacked and thought no more of it. This would happen before anyone in the hospital had got up, so they would not have known the crates had moved. Timmy filched a clean sheet from the laundry that was located in one of the out buildings. This building was normally locked but Timmy had noticed a window open, so with the help of the milk crates, had gained entry. It was a good job there was a moon out, because it was very dark inside, but he found what he wanted and was soon back in his room and making up his bed.

They thought they had got away with it, until a visiting tradesman asked the gardener if the roof leaked. There on the roof looking for all the world like a tarpaulin, was the sheet, draped over one corner. The Matron did not think it was a tarpaulin, because as she was heard to say later on, "You don't get many bright white tarpaulins." She guessed quite correctly it was a bed sheet. Her next guess was also an inspired one. She cornered Timmy. "I spilt something on it," said Timmy. "So I put it on the windowsill to dry, and the wind blew it away. You know how windy it was last night, don't you? I'll climb up and get it if you like?" He volunteered. This offer was turned down. Timmy was quite pleased, because he was not really fond of heights. The gardener had stated, "There is no way in the world I'm going up on that roof." So a builder with a ladder was hired. No one ever did ask why there was a bit of chair attached to the sheet.

Another time they experimented with the fire escape. This rope contraption was situated in an empty room almost opposite the boy's room. Timmy said, "They were within their rights to practice, so they would know what to do if there was a fire." He was of course quite right, but this was on a dark night and they should have all been asleep. There wasn't a volunteer for the first run, so once again a chair was bought into use. Remembering the back had broken off the chair used for the parachute, the harness was put around the seat, and lowered over the parapet. All went well until it got stuck on the windowsill of the room below, but with a bit of wiggling of the rope, they got it over the obstacle and it reached the ground. When they hauled it back up the same problem occurred and the same method was used to pass the jutting out windowsill, but then the top back of the chair got stuck in the top of the window recess. The boys were only a few feet above the top of the window and could not lean out far enough to free the chair, they tried swing it but it was to no avail. The chair was then lowered to the windowsill and the rope was secured to make sure it stayed there.

They then went looking for a broom or something similar to push the rope away from the wall and clear of the window recess. This was a sound idea, but before it could be put into practice, footsteps were heard on the twisting stairs leading up to the attic. It was the auxiliary nurse whose room was next door. There was another person with her and the boys only just made it back to their beds, before the two women walked passed the open doorway. The light was put on in the nurse's room, but the door was not shut, the boy's could hear them talking. After what seemed ages one of the women left, they could hear her going down the stairs. The only trouble was, the door was still open with light streaming across the passage and into the room with the fire escape. Timmy thought, she must close it soon, but while waiting, one by one they all fell asleep.

When nurse Popeye drew her curtains next morning, she was quite surprised to see a chair sitting on her windowsill.

About a week later, the three boys were in their attic room getting ready for bed; it was early bed because they were still being punished for the fire escape episode and other things. They were dragging it out as usual, when nurse Popeye came clumping up the stairs and into their room. Timmy thought he was in for another scolding for something he had done, or had not done. But all she did was take a blanket out of the cupboard at the far end of the room. As she went out through the doorway she turned and said, "Timmy you're going home tomorrow." Timmy couldn't believe his ears.

"Tomorrow?" He said, with an amazed look on his face.

"Yes tomorrow, your parents are coming for you at lunchtime and not before time." She said this with feeling, as she clumped back down the stairs. "I knew that boy would be trouble from the moment I set eyes on him." She had said this to other members of the staff many times over, when describing their first encounter in the kitchen of Timmy's home.

Timmy did not know how he felt, he wanted to laugh, and he wanted to cry, at the same time. What he found most incredible was, he had been here for well over a year and they had not given him any warning or inkling that he was about to be discharged. He thought they would tell him, 'You'll be going home in a few weeks', or something like that, not leave it to late one night and just say, "Your going home tomorrow." In fact if it hadn't been for the blankets he probably wouldn't have been told that night.

In the morning Timmy was so excited he could hardly eat his breakfast. The teacher looked in and asked him to come and see her before he left for home. When the others had gone to school, he went up to his room with one of the staff to pack. He had a small battered case but his meagre belongings nowhere filled it, even with a few of his favourite books it was still half empty. He had quite a lot of books, most he did not want to take home, these he took down to the small library. They were mostly novels and he had read them all. He could not understand people who would read a story book several times. With his packing done and wearing a shirt, socks and shoes he was now free to wait for his parents.

He walked around the hospital talking to the staff. He was of course, restless and impatient, every time he passed the big clock in the hallway only a few minutes had gone by. To kill time he walked up to the top of the field and sat on a fallen tree trunk. It was a beautiful view from here, but the most important thing was, it overlooked the lane, so he would be able to see his parents walking along the lane, long before they arrived at the gate.

Timmy was quite happy to sit all alone on the log. He contemplated his stay in the hospital and the things that had happened to him, and the things he had done; some of which he was not very proud of. But his life was already beginning to change, just to be alone as he was now was a luxury, it was one of the many things he had missed. Solitude was a rare commodity in an institution like this. On the last few visits from his parents he had walked with them to the bus stop. Primarily so he could spend as much time with them as possible, but walking back alone was something he really enjoyed. This rare solitude had to be savoured, it would take him an hour or even longer to get back and the beauty of it was; he was not missed by the hospital staff or anyone else, because they thought he was with his visitors.

He thought about home and his sisters, of the three of them he had only seen one in the last year. She was three years older than him and had contracted the same disease though she was not hospitalised, because as the doctor had said 'her body is fighting it naturally'. His youngest sister was really too small to make the journey, and as the disease was contagious, it was decided she would not visit him. The oldest sister had been away from home longer than Timmy and was in a sanatorium for adults, situated in a range of hills on the other side of the county. Timmy had been taken there once, but they had not been able to meet, because of a strict no children rule. This sanatorium was housed in a beautiful building and the interior was as opulent as Timmy's establishment was bleak.

He thought about his parents and how they had coped with two children at home and visiting two in different hospitals. To visit either of these establishments takes a whole day with many bus changes and in Timmy's case, quite a long walk. It was probably just as well they could only visit him once a month. He was lost to the outside world as he sat there musing, a boy all alone sitting on a fallen tree, deep in thought. At the back of his mind he could hear his name being called, there it was again, getting louder and more persistent. He shook his head and stood up. He then realised he had not been dreaming, the voices were not at the back of his mind, it was his parents and one of the staff. They were at the back door of the hospital calling for him to come down out of the field. He had not seen them arrive, the sole reason for sitting on the tree trunk was to see them before they arrived. He could not believe his eyes, how could he have missed them, how long had he been sitting there? Maybe they had come early. He raced down the field towards them, all deep thoughts now scattered to the wind. It was the Matron who was with his parents and as he arrived out of breath, she turned to them and said. "You see he doesn't want to leave."

"Oh yes I do!" said Timmy and as his father already had his suitcase, he took hold of his parent's hands and marched them down to the gate. They were halfway down the path when he suddenly thought of the teacher; he had promised to see her before he left. He turned and ran back up the path shouting to his parents.

"I won't be a minute," as he disappeared around the corner and up the slope to the school. The school was a wooden building, a bit like a Swiss Chalet in style. At one end there were big folding doors, windows at the top and plain wood at the bottom. Set in these large folding doors was a smaller door for use when the big ones were closed. Today the folding doors were closed, because there was a stiff wind. It was very quiet in the school, so when Timmy burst in sending the door back with a crash, every one, including the teacher, jumped. He ran over to the teacher, shaking her by the hand he almost shouted, "I'm going home now, miss."

"I've got something for you," she said, turned round and reaching under the desk came up with a brown paper parcel. Why on earth has she bothered to wrap it? Thought Timmy, because it was of course a book. She then did something completely uncharacteristic and so surprised Timmy he was speechless and not a little embarrassed. As she was giving him the book, she wrapped her arms around him and gave him a hug. She then pushed him away and held him at arms length, a hand on each shoulder. He had never seen her with such a huge smile or grin, it seemed to take up the whole of her face. It seemed to Timmy she had great difficulty in regaining control of her face and mouth, but when she did manage it, she said, "Timmy I would like to say, never change, but of course you will, so what I will say is, enjoy life because I'm quite sure you will and I am so glad to have met you." With that

she turned him round and pushed him towards the door. The children were now standing up and had opened the big doors. As he passed they slapped him on the back and shook his hand. He ran down the slope and at the bottom turned and looked back. The children were all in the doorway waving and shouting their goodbyes. With one last wave he disappeared through the archway and raced round the main hospital building and down the path. At last he was going home, he was so glad to be going home;

so why was there a tear in his eye? His parents were waiting impatiently by the gate, the Matron still with them.

"You see, I told you he doesn't want to go home?" said the Matron. Timmy gave the book to his mother to carry and taking her free hand and that of his father's, he dragged them out into the lane.

'No one will ever know how much I've been waiting for this day', he said, quietly to himself. His parents looked back at the hospital several times as they went down the lane; knowing that in all probability they would never see this building again. Timmy didn't, he was only looking forward, he was going to try and forget this place ever existed.

He just wanted to go home.

"That was a long story, Granddad," said Stuart. "Was that place really as bad as you told it, Granddad, and did Timmy really dislike so much?"

"Yes, I think it was a fair description of the place and the regime. Although Timmy didn't like it, he made the most of it and survived, as did most of the other inmates. Later in life, when he looked back, he realised they were only trying to make him better and it had to be an authoritative regime, but why did it have to be so harsh?"

Home

The grandfather and two boys had been to watch a special steam train as it passed through the next village and were now sitting in the kitchen musing on the day's event.

"Were all the trains steam trains when you were young, Granddad?" said James.

"Yes they were mostly steam trains, though diesels were coming in, and there were of course electric trains, but they did not run in this area," said the old man.

James thought about this and then said, "Those two boys, Tom and Timmy, did they ever go on trains?"

"Yes, they had both been on trains, but not very often; you see they lived a long way from the nearest station and that line only went from Highbridge to Evercreech Junction, so a lot of changes were required to do a journey of any significance."

"Talking of Tom and Timmy Granddad, can you tell us another story about them?" Said James.

"That's a good idea," said Stuart, "what I want to know is how Timmy got on when he left that hospital."

"And so do I," said James. "I want to know if Timmy and Tom ever got back to being great friends again?"

"OK," said the grandfather. "But there is not too much to tell about Timmy at this stage, because when he got home, it was almost as if phase three had started in his young life.

When he first came home, his mother found him rather difficult to deal with. It was as if he was a stranger;

he was definitely a different boy to the one that had gone into hospital. Timmy was now very quick tempered, independent, tended to be secretive, he was protective of any possessions he had and was rather belligerent. In many ways he was also rather childish, or young for his age, though this did not last for long and he was soon to grow up very quickly. He was of course at the beginning of adulthood.

It was early evening when Timmy got home. As well as his sisters and immediate family there were a few other people in his house, all adults. They shook his hand and he was glad to see them, but what he really wanted was to get out and meet his friends. At last he was told he could go out. He ran up the path, through the gate and out on to the road, he was of course going to see Tom first, but then he stopped in the middle of the road; he just stood there for a while, a great sense of freedom flowing over him, so much so it almost overwhelmed him. It was quite a few minutes before he continued up the road at a more sedate pace. He then thought about Tom's rather difficult visit when he was in hospital. Would they still be the great friends they once were? Timmy knocked on the back door of Tom's house feeling a little bit apprehensive, he and his friends had always used the back door, because most other people knocked on the front door. Tom and the rest of his family would know it was probably one of his mates, so if he was in, Tom would always answer the back door. The door was torn open and out flew Tom; he literally jumped on Timmy who almost fell over.

"I thought it would be you!" shouted Tom. "I've been waiting in for you all day." When they had disentangled themselves Tom kept touching, holding and even punching Timmy, as if to make sure he was really there.

"I'm so glad you're back," said Tom, dragging Timmy

in to meet the rest of his family. They then went out and met as many of there mutual friends as possible.

"We can't do much tonight Timmy," said Tom. "But if you have nothing planned for tomorrow what would you like to do?" Timmy thought for a minute. "I don't think there is any thing planned for tomorrow," replied Timmy. "What I would really like if it's a nice day; would be to walk up to Butliegh Monument."

"OK," said Tom. "If the weather is all right we'll all meet tomorrow, about half past nine on the crossroads." Butleigh Monument was a lighthouse type of construction built on a range of wooded hills, these woods opened out in places to reveal quite breath taking views. Timmy's mother was a bit apprehensive when he told her of his plans for Sunday, because the walk was rather long and he was not supposed to do too much exercise. In fact when he started back to school he was not allowed to do any sport or visit the Gym. Swimming and cycling were also supposed to be prohibited. His mother decided quite wisely, it would be useless to forbid him to go with the other boy's, so in the morning she made him some sandwiches, for this excursion would take all day. With his sandwiches and a bottle of water he met the others on the crossroads as planned, and the five of them set off on their walk. Timmy was glad they were all wearing short trousers, because he would not be getting long trousers until he started back to school. It was an easy pace they set, five abreast across the road; they could do this because in those days there was very little traffic. The easy pace was for Timmy's benefit though he didn't realise it. As they walked along the road, the talk, wit, jokes and the general camaraderie, was really exhilarating to Timmy; he had almost forgotten what it was like to be with a group of people his own age. He was enthralled by the conversations and how the talk twisted and turned over a huge range of topics, some of which went completely over his head. What did surprise him most was their interest in girls. His friends of course had gone on a year or so, since they were last together. Timmy's existence in the hospital had been in something like a time warp. In all his time there, he had not read a newspaper or listened to a radio, even comics were banned. His only contact with the outside world had been through his friend the teacher and his parents who could only visit, once a month. This lack of contact with the outside world and his long association with younger children, meant that on his release, he was not as worldly, or grown up as his peers; though he was soon to catch up. He confided in Tom his fears they would not be friends when he got out.

"You are daft," said Tom, putting his arm over Timmy's shoulder. "We'll always be friends." Together they walked arms across each others shoulders for quite a while, until rude comments were made by the others in the group.

About three quarters of the way through their journey they stopped to have a sandwich and a drink. The water that was left over was then hidden for the return journey, they would be thirsty then and they didn't want to carry bottles while messing about in the woods and on the hills. They had a great time, met a group of boys from another village who were dirt tracking on their bikes and picked wild strawberries.

"These strawberries are so small it would take all day to pick a cupful," said Tom, but Timmy thought they were very nice and picked as many as he could, he collected them in his handkerchief and took them back to where he had hidden his last jam sandwich. His sandwich was now covered in ants, but Timmy didn't mind, he picked the ants out and replaced them with the little strawberry's, he thought it was the best sandwich he had ever tasted.

Timmy went back up the hill to look at the monument, although he had been there many times in the past, he had never really studied it, or read the inscription on the side. He was glad he did, for inside the railings was a notice stating: 'This monument will be open to the public, for one day only'. It then gave a date that was several months away. The fee was a bit steep, but Timmy knew he would raise it somehow or the other, because from the top of the monument, the view must be fantastic. 'I must tell Tom'. He said to himself as he raced back down the hill to join the others who were starting back for home. They started back early mainly because they were thirsty, but it was on the insistence of Tom who was thinking of his friend. He thought to stay any longer might be too much for Timmy, on his first day home. On the way back the scintillating talk and wit was not so obvious. After such an active day, they were all a bit tired, Timmy was obviously more tired than most and he was at the back as they straggled along in single file, for this part of the journey was on a narrow path. Timmy was not overly tired, but he would be the first to admit he was looking forward to getting home so he could have a rest. As they walked he mused on his first full day of freedom. It had been fantastic, one of the best he could remember and this of course was only the first day home. Life did look good to Timmy at that moment.

About three quarters of the way home, Timmy looked back to the monument standing out high above the trees and then towards their village; when he caught up with the others who were waiting for him he said to Tom, "This must be one of the few walks of any length that is in an almost straight line."

"What on earth do you mean?" said Tom. "Well if you think about it," replied Timmy. "We have walked along roads, lanes, droves, footpaths and across fields, all in a dead straight line. When there is a turning in the road we go straight on across a field or along a drove or path. I bet there are not many walks from our village where you can do this."

"I reckon I could walk anywhere in a straight line if I wanted too," said Tom. "Of course you couldn't," replied Timmy "Lots of things could get in your way." There then ensued a general discussion, sometimes quite heated, but Tom was so sure of himself, he turned to Timmy and said, "Name me a walk from the village and I'll do it in a straight line."

"OK," said Timmy. "I'll bet you can't walk in a straight line from the village to Tor Hill?"

"Done," replied Tom. "I'll do it next Sunday."

By the time they got home, Timmy was very tired; he even fell asleep over his tea. He went to bed as soon as he had finished his food and did not get up until teatime the next day. His mother was very worried and vowed he would not do another excursion like that again for a long time, or not until he was really well. The rather childish wager between Tom and Timmy that was for nothing material, only Tom's bravado; seemed to catch the imagination of a surprisingly lot of people and as the weekend drew near many spoke to Tom about it. This included many adults. Tom loved the attention and even suggested he would do it in about an hour and a half, though time was not part of the bet. People spoke to Timmy as well about this bizarre competition, many asked why he hadn't picked a harder walk, because most of the route would be over the open moors.

"Well if you think about it," Timmy replied to several of them. "There has to be a prominent landmark; if you don't have the object or place you are walking towards in view all the time, how will you, or any one else, know if you are walking in a straight line?" But the fact was, the walk to Tor Hill was the first one Timmy had thought of and anyway he was rather hoping Tom would do it, even though he didn't think he would. A competition committee had been formed and Timmy was the Hon Sec. He wrote down the rules of the first and only meeting only to lose them shortly afterwards. The rules were quite simple. The committee will walk with Tom to make sure he stays on a straight line, though they of course can go around obstacles. The committee's judgement shall be final. If the committee deem that Tom has gone off the straight line he will have lost the competition. The next rule caused a lot of argument and was only passed on a majority decision. When Tom comes to an obstacle he can take twenty steps either way to get round it, but must get back on the straight line as soon as he has passed it. Timmy proposed this rule, because as he said, "You can't expect Tom to go over the top of a house or barn, can you?" The last rule was the starting place and it was decided to be Tom's back door.

"In some ways, it's a pity about the twenty steps rule," said Timmy. "When Tom starts from his back door he can do twenty steps to one side and go out the gate. It would have been funny if he had to go through the flower garden and over the front hedge. I don't think his parents would have been very pleased." There seemed to be a growing excitement in this little band of friends as the weekend drew near. Timmy's mother thought they were quite mad. When Sunday dawned the weather was atrocious, it was teeming with rain and blowing a gale. "You're not going out in that!" said Timmy's mother, and it was quite obvious to all; Tom's walk was not going to take place on that day. The following Sunday was, if anything worse, and so it was three weeks before this rather silly competition took place.

In the meantime Timmy's oldest sister came home. Now this posed a problem. Their house only had three bedrooms and because of the contagious nature of their diseases, they had to have rooms on their own. It was decided that the two unaffected sisters would have one room, his eldest sister would have Timmy's old room and Timmy would sleep in a chalet in the garden.

This so-called chalet was provided by the local council, but when the workmen had put it up, Timmy thought it looked just like a garden shed. It was square in shape, with a roof sloping towards the back and double sliding windows on each side. The whole of the front opened up having double half doors; above these stable-like doors, was a canvas-covered frame that was hinged at the top and opened up like a flap, or a canopy. This flap or canopy had a big tear in it about four feet long, which the workmen repaired with some sort of sticky tape. They said it was only a temporary repair job and they would report it to the council. True, a man from the council did come round to inspect it, but it was never repaired, and the sticky tape soon fell off. Timmy didn't mind using the shed; in fact he rather liked it, spending a lot of time in it when, for some reason or the other, he could not go out. He could not see much difference in having a bedroom in the house or in the garden. The only thing he found a nuisance were the cats, he would quite often wake to find several in his shed, he didn't even mind that but it was when they started yowling and fighting he would get mad, only then would he get up and chase them out.

His living in a shed created a lot of interest, when he went back to school. The story got around that he lived in a shed on his own in the middle of the moor. Timmy was quite sure that Tom was the instigator of this story, though Tom always denied it. Later, instead of knocking on the door his friends would often throw stones or mud at his shed to see if he was in.

'I'm being paid back for what I did to Albert Bush all those years ago', he thought after a particularly noisy bombardment.

The third Sunday turned out to be a beautiful day and the committee met outside of Tom's house at the pre-arranged time, but Tom did not come out. "I think he's scared," said David. "He knows he can't do it." Timmy went to the house and knocked on the door. It was answered by Tom, who beckoned him in. "I won't be few minutes," said Tom. "Come into the kitchen, my sister is giving me a hand."

"That should do it." She said as they walked into the kitchen and handed Tom a couple of sacks. These sacks had been folded in half long ways and roughly sewn in that position; with her help they were tied on Tom's legs, with leather straps and bits of string. Timmy looked on in amazement; to him they looked almost like chaps that cowboys wore. When they had finished Tom put on an old coat that was ripped in several places, picked up his fishing bag and hung it from his shoulder, then put on a pair of leather gloves that looked much too big for him.

"Right," he said to Timmy. "I'm ready." Together they left the house and walked up onto the road. Almost all of the committee and a few others that were going on the trip, were sat on the grass verge. Some had taken their shirts off because even at this time of the morning it was warm. It promised to be a very hot day indeed. When Tom came out of his house, there was a burst of laughter. This laughter became almost hysterical when he took off his gloves, opened his fishing bag and took out an old Sou'wester, which he proceeded to put on and tie the strings tightly under his chin. There was so much hilarity some had to wipe away the tears of laughter from their eyes and others were actually rolling on the floor. There were lots of comments about cowboys and where was his horse, and did he think it was going to snow, or rain, many thought he might get picked up as a tramp or vagrant.

Tom didn't seem to mind and joined in with the laughter, but after a while he said, "Well let's get started then." And so this little band set of across the first field, with Tom leading the way in his bazaar outfit. It soon became apparent why Tom had dressed in this way, because the first hedge was very big indeed, it was overgrown and full of brambles, good for blackberry's but a formidable obstacle with a barbed wire fence to start with. Tom climbed up the fence then, standing on one of the posts, launched himself over the hedge. He only made it halfway, but his leap had taken him to the top and with much heaving and struggling, finally managed to land on the grass, in an orchard the other side.

The committee meanwhile had gone through the gate and were waiting for him and together they all trooped across the orchard. The next hedge was similar to the last, even having a barbed wire fence to start with. Tom used the same method to get over it, but after only two hedges he was starting to feel tired and it was taking much longer than he thought it would. Through the next orchard they walked, over a small fence and hedge before coming to the next hindrance to Tom's straight line. This was a row of cottages at an angle to the proposed route and even with the twenty steps leeway Tom was in trouble. If he went to the left it would take him through the front garden of the first cottage and part of the second. If he went to the right he would have to go through the back and side garden of the last, then jump over the hedge onto the road. Tom's mind was made up for him when an upstairs window was thrown open in the first cottage and the occupant demanded to know what they were up too. While the committee went back out through the gate, Tom ran along the back of the cottages, over the fence of the last, through the vegetables and jumped at the hedge. He did not make it all the way over, but landed on the top, this was not an overgrown field hedge, it was a well kept garden hedge and supported his weight, so all he had to do, was roll over onto the road down below. When the others had caught him up, Tom was rested and ready to move on, but he was nursing a grazed elbow from his fall onto the road. The next few hedges and ditches were no trouble to Tom, but there was looming a problem none of them had foreseen. There were two large farms in the way, no one had realised they would be in the line between the village and Tor Hill. The farmer of the second was not very friendly at all, mainly because they had raided his orchards several times. The committee decided quite wisely they would take a large detour around both of these farms, but warned Tom they would be watching him. Of course they could not watch him the whole of the time and even when they could see him, they could not tell if he was keeping to the line. When they met on the other side of the farms Tom was covered in mud. He told them his tactics had been speed, so he had discarded his protective clothing, chosen a time when he thought nobody was looking and ran across the front garden of the first farm. After collecting his breath in the orchards between the two farms, he just ran in and around the farm buildings of the second; the only trouble being the sloping concrete farmyard. When he had run across it he had slipped and fallen in the muck. So that wasn't just mud on him, no-wonder he smelt a bit and he had cut his knee as well. The cottages, hedges, orchards and farms of the village were now behind them, in front for the next few miles were the open sedge moors. These moors that had once been marshy bog and flooded on some of the higher spring tides. The drainage of the moors had been started by the monks many years ago. They had used a system of ditches and drains called rhynes to achieve this and some of them were very big indeed, these were the next obstacles for Tom. The first few were not too big, though there was a lot of water in them from the recent heavy rains. The whole committee managed to jump them with Tom, some with only a varied degree of success, but, they then came across a rhyne that was much to big to jump and the committee had to make a large detour before they found a bridge. As for Tom he was well prepared, he just took his clothes off, put them in his fishing bag and threw it over the rhyne. He plunged into the water and swam across. It must have been cold, because even after drying himself with a towel he had in his bag and redressing, he was shivering and looked blue. He strolled across the field, trying to look nonchalant as he waited for the others to catch up. This set the pattern for the journey over the moors and it began to look more and more likely that this competition would be won.

After the low open moors there was a slight rise to yet

another farm and once again the committee elected to give it a wide birth, telling Tom they would meet him on the main road that divided the moors from the beginning of the Tor. Tom decided to use the same tactics as he had used for the other farms and go for speed. The farm looked exceptionally quiet which was not surprising this being about midday on a Sunday and Tom thought it would be a piece of cake, in fact he was clear of all the buildings and heading for a barbed wire and chain link fence before he heard the ferocious babble of growling and barking. This farm had dogs and they were giving chase. Before the arrival of the dogs, Tom had thought the fence was an obstacle and he was wondering how he was going to get over it, now he was so glad it was there and threw himself up over it, just as the first of the three dogs reached him. He teetered on the top and to an onlooker it might have looked as if he would fall back, but with those ferocious teeth below there is know way Tom would have fallen back, but as he dropped to the other side he could hear his trousers rip and received quite a bad cut on the top of one leg.

He raced across a small field and jumped a large ditch, or tried to because he was not quite successful and the water was almost up to his waist as he struggled out the other side. Tom looked back at the dogs, he was glad that they seemed to be quite stupid, because they were still at the fence snarling and barking when there was an open gate on one side of the paddock. He collected his breath and trudged up towards the main road where he was meeting the others. Here the walking was good, the grass was mown down very short as if they were school playing fields, he could see the cars going along the main road and thought all the major obstacles were now out of the way. He did not know how wrong he could be. Between the well-manicured fields and the road was a small oblong shaped, tree-lined field, with an unkempt hedge. In the field were a dozen or so chicken houses and it seemed to Tom, they housed thousands of chickens. To keep these chicken in their compound, thin wire mesh or chicken wire of about ten feet in height had been nailed to the trees, all around the field, on the inside of the hedge. This field was strung out along the road so Tom only had to cross it in the narrow direction, the only trouble was, he could hear lots of banging and unchicken-like noises coming from inside the compound. He climbed a tree to assess the situation and there, mending, or doing something to one of the nearest chicken houses, was a man and a boy. Almost opposite the tree Tom had climbed he could hear and see through a gap in the hedge, his comrades messing about on the road waiting for him. Tom decided to go for it and climbed out along a branch. Choosing his time when the man and the boy's backs were turned, he dropped quietly down on the grass. Well, he thought it was going to be quiet but he sent chickens squawking, clucking and flying in all directions as he sprinted across the field. There was a shout from the man as he dropped his tools and gave chase, but Tom was quick and was halfway up the chicken wire on the far side before the man had hardly started.

The only trouble was, chicken wire is bendy and stretches, the spot that Tom had chosen could not have been worse. This was the only area where there was a large gap in the trees and consequently the netting wire strung between was rather loose. Tom had chosen right bang in the middle, as he climbed the netting wire, it bent back towards the field and the further he went up the worse it got, so much so that when he was near the top he was actually upside down and only a few feet from the ground. He dropped off the wire on to his head, this did not seem to hurt much, because as he jumped up he shouted to the others "Help me quick!" This whole little episode had been watched by the committee in an almost mesmerised fashion, Timmy was the first to react, he had noticed that the netting wire was loose at the bottom and rushed over and pulled it up.

"Underneath, quick Tom!" He shouted. They were only just in time, as they rolled down the bank onto the road, the man arrived at the fence. All the children ran down the road, with the exception of Tom, who could of course, only cross the road, this he did and jumped into a large laurel hedge, disappearing from sight. The man had now been joined by the boy as he peered through the gap in the hedge, he said to the young lad, "Do you know those children, boy?"

"No, Dad, never seen them before," replied the boy.

"Well," said the man taking his cap off and scratching his head. "I think the one who ran across the field is a bit doolally, the others ran down the road but he has just jumped into the Henderson's hedge. When I've fixed this fence I think I'll go over and have a word with Henderson."

The committee were now at the foot of the Tor and, walking along the boundary hedge, found Tom waiting for them. So he had done it, there was nothing to stop him now, just an ordinary climb up the hill. They sat for a while swapping tales, Tom telling them of his adventures. After they had rested, all but Timmy started to climb the hill. He had promised his mother he would not go up the hill and now he was glad he had because he was feeling a bit whacked. It had been arranged for him to be to be picked up at the bottom of the Tor by someone from the village, who had a motorcycle and sidecar. His mother did not want him to get in the state he had been in on his first day home. He sat down on the grass and it wasn't long before he was having a nap on that warm sunny day.

Timmy was woken by the return of the others. He heard them long before they came into sight. A heated argument seemed to be taking place. So much so that when they came to where Timmy was sitting they almost walked past him. It was Tom who stopped and sat down beside him and then the others came back and sat down as well. Tom looked furious. He started to tell Timmy what had happened, but was interrupted so many times it was a long time before Timmy got the gist of the argument.

It transpired that when they had left Timmy to climb the hill, all were in good spirits, cracking jokes and telling stories as they climbed. They were about three quarters of way up the steep side of the Tor, when someone looked up and realised they were going to miss the tower on the top of the hill, and it was going to be by some considerable margin.

So, in the opinion of many, Tom had lost his bet. Some thought he had been deliberately led off course and Tom thought so too. "What do you think Timmy?" He said. "Well" said Timmy, "Although I don't know if it was a deliberate ploy, or not, you won anyway. The bet I had with you, was to walk in a straight line from your house to Tor Hill, and reach it you did; I didn't say you had to climb it." This verdict did not seem to satisfy anyone and there was much bickering for most of the return journey, though the heat seemed to have gone out of the argument by the time they had reached the village and met up with Timmy. It had now changed to good natured bantering.

Tom trudged into the kitchen and slumped down in a chair.

"It's been a great day, Mum." He said. "It's great having Timmy back, I haven't enjoyed myself so much for ages, and we do seem to have fun when we're together."

"Mmm," said his mother eyeing her dishevelled son, with his scratched face, grazed elbow, blooded knee and ripped trousers, through the rip a large cut in his flesh was visible. He was covered in mud, if mud was all it was, because he smelt terrible. "Mmmm," she said again, she wasn't totally convinced it was so great, having Timmy back home.

The following morning found Tom and Timmy sitting together in the morning assembly of the large school they now attended in the local town. There were several hundred in the hall and they sat on the floor cross-legged in rows. After the prayers and a hymn came the normal announcements about school activities and the like. These were made by a teacher standing at a Dias or lectern on the small stage. The headmaster, with papers in his hand replaced this teacher and addressed the school.

"I believe that one of our village contingency's had a rather interesting competition over the weekend. How did you get on Tom?" Tom stood up and said, "I did it, Sir." Then sat down.

In the same row sat most of the committee and one of them jumped up and said, "He didn't, Sir." And sat down.

Timmy jumped up and almost shouted, "He did, Sir." Then another of the committee jumped up and actually did shout, "He didn't, sir." All this jumping up and down from a row near the front of the hall resulted in gales of laughter from the rest of the congregation and from the teachers up on the stage. When the head teacher had restored order, he said with a laugh, "I was thinking of doing something like that for the school sports, but if it causes so much controversy I will have to think again."

One of the boys in the row put up his hand.

"Yes John?" said the headmaster. John stood up.

"Please Sir," he said. "It was Timmy that had the original bet with Tom and if Timmy says Tom has won, then he has won."

"Enough, enough" said the headmaster, "I don't want to hear another word on the subject, though I did hear that Timmy had something to do with it. Stand up Timmy." Timmy was shocked. Was he in trouble already? He had only been back at school for fifteen minutes. He stood up as requested, with a sense of foreboding and feeling rather self-conscious in his new long trousers. The headmaster said, "Not all of you will know Timmy, because he has been away from school for eighteen months or probably a lot longer." He looked down at his notes. "No, it is almost two years and a lot of that time he has spent in hospital. He has not fully recovered but, has chosen to come back to school. Although, he will not be able to take part in sports; PE, or anything too physical, he will be able to participate in all other aspects of school life. So let's give him a round of applause."

As the clapping started, Timmy felt even more embarrassed, he could feel his face burning and was glad to sit down; even his ears were tingling. This was the last thing he had wanted. He thought he would be able to slip back in to school, almost unnoticed and take up where he had left off.

And so Timmy had settled back into home life and was now settling down at school. His life was almost back to normal.

Tom and Timmy's escapades continued, but they were now teenagers; with a growing awareness and appreciation of girls. With one or two exceptions their escapades were now almost wholly of another nature. Some of these I might tell you when you are older.